The Chevelle roared to life. Hearing the motor rumble and the garage door open, Mary tossed her school bag onto her back, grabbed her lunch pail, and hurried out the door to catch her mother. Fifteen minutes later than the day before, and sure to get another lecture, Mary opened the door on the passenger side. They were late because she'd had trouble getting out of bed, even though her mother had woken her three times.

"Where's your sweater, Mary?" Eva Kelly asked.

"It's going to be warm later," Mary argued.

"Go inside and get one." Her mother's voice rose.

Mary tossed the book bag and pail onto the seat and rushed back inside. The dampness in the air on the chilly September morning made the smell of rotting leaves even more intense. Eva revved the engine a few times to urge Mary along and because she liked the sound.

When Mary returned, carrying a navy-blue sweater instead of wearing it, Eva said, "Put it on, Mary. You will catch a cold."

It never did any good to complain about wearing the sweater or the same outfit every day, so Mary held her tongue. After this year, she would no longer have to follow the strict dress code at Saint Catherine's Catholic School. Plaid skirts, a white cotton blouse, and a navy sweater. The only thing Mary could change to stand out was the color of her knee socks. White, blue, or gray were the only colors allowed, though. Failure to follow the rules was grounds for expulsion.

The 1972 Chevelle rumbled out of the driveway. Mary loved the sound of the engine and the yellow-gold strips that went down the black hood. What excited her the most was that the car would be hers someday.

"Tell me the story of how you got this car," Mary urged.

"You've heard the story hundreds of times," Mrs. Kelly said.

Wide-eyed and interested, Mary tucked her auburn locks behind her ears and smiled. "Please, Mom."

"You're only asking to avoid a lecture for staying up past your bedtime," her mother said, stating the obvious.

"But you said I could," Mary argued.

The entire family had enjoyed the talent show. Her father and mother sat on the couch with Mary ogling in the middle. Right from the beginning, Mary picked a person she believed would win and stuck with them—rarely, her choices in the previous programs didn't make it to the finals. Mary thought she would make a better judge. The program got pushed back an hour from its regularly scheduled time and ended at eleven o'clock. Worked up and disappointed that the heartthrob boy singer had lost to an equally gifted girl singer, Mary hadn't shut her eyes until after midnight.

"Yes, against my better judgment." It had been the series finale, and Mrs. Kelly hadn't thought one night would hurt. "Too bad Adam didn't win."

"Yeah, but my choice made it to number two," Mary answered proudly.

"You're good at picking." Eva smiled. "Look in my purse. I have something for you."

"What, Mom?" Mary asked as she peeked inside.

"They're for after school only." Eva gave her the "I know you'll try to sneak them" look.

With a broad smile, Mary nodded and placed the bag of M&M's in one of the many pockets in her pack and zipped it closed. "Thanks, Mom."

Mary watched her mother shift into each gear with ease. Someday, her hand would be on the red ball with the number three in the center. Her mother's hand had worn off half the paint. Mary wondered if she would be able to drive as well as her mother. A memory of what had happened at their family's auto repair shop a day prior filled her head.

Mary had sat her backpack and lunch pail on the floor next to her father's desk and headed to the car in the first bay. "Hi, Dad."

Mary startled him. He lifted his head, bumped it on the hood, then dropped the screwdriver. "Where did you come from?"

"It fell underneath," Mary said when her father scanned the area in front of the car. As if second nature, she walked to one of the many metal tool chests next to the wall and pulled a straight-blade screwdriver, knowing instinctively what size and type he needed to adjust a carburetor.

The car's color and body style looked similar to the Chevelle—black with two gold stripes on the hood and trunk.

"What kind of car is this?" Mary asked, knowing it was a classic.

"It's a 1969 Buick Skylark," her father replied. "Where in the heck is Shane?"

Mary shrugged and watched him turn the screw clockwise until it was seated. "Can I help?" Mary asked eagerly. "Sort of looks like Mom's Chevelle. Is it as fast?"

"Nah, nothing can beat Mom's car," he said with a laugh. Mary couldn't tell if he was being truthful. His smile made it doubtful. "Start it up." He motioned toward the car for her to climb behind the wheel.

Mary beamed, almost skipping to the door. Once inside, she moved the seat forward, put her right foot on the break and the left on the clutch, and turned the key. When the car began to purr, it told Mary her father had adjusted the carburetor's jets to the right speed. Instinctively, from the years of spending her afternoons after school at the garage, she knew a mechanic needed to set the idle speed between seven hundred and nine hundred RPMs. At twelve, she lacked the vast knowledge her father had to make the repairs, but her ears were minstrels of the mechanical world. Her father often called her The Mozart of Timing.

"Cut the engine!" her father yelled.

Mary turned off the ignition, removed her left foot then the right, and hopped out.

"Shane was helping me," her father said as he looked around.

"Hey, Mary," the young recruit said, appearing out of nowhere. Except for the smear of grease on his coveralls, they looked unused. The only spot clean on her father was the upper back.

"Hey," Mary mumbled. After a short wave, she gave him a questionable stare. Shane had taken her job of helping Dad the past spring when business picked up. *Why did I have to get the screwdriver? Isn't that his job?*

"I was helping a customer," Shane said as if reading Mary's thoughts.

After wiping his hands, her father tucked the rag into the rear pocket of his coveralls. "Come here, Mary. I have something to show you."

He told Shane he could leave after sweeping up, then he led Mary into the office. The door barely cleared the chair in front of his desk. Invoices and car parts covered the top. He opened a drawer in the heavy gray metal desk and pulled out a small box—the outside covered with greasy fingerprints.

"What is it?" Mary asked.

"It took me a while, but I finally found one."

"Found what, Dad?" Mary peeked inside the box and saw only green Styrofoam peanuts.

"Go ahead." Her dad gestured for her to reach inside. The green foam fell out as she shuffled through the box's contents. When her fingers found something cold, hard, and round, she wrapped her hand around it and pulled a new ball for the gearshift from the box.

"It's for your mother's birthday next week." An excited smile formed on his face. He was almost giddy. "Do you think she'll like it?"

Most women wanted flowers, jewelry, or a night on the town. Not Mary's mother. A set of new tires, chrome rims, or a freshly waxed car made her mother beam. A wild smile appeared on Mary's face.

"Yes, can I give it to her?" Mary bounced. The bouncing stopped, and the happiness left her face. "But I have no money?"

"Let's say it's from the both of us."

Mary wrapped her arms around him. He held her at bay. "We don't want your mother upset with you or me for getting grease on your uniform. And don't tell her I let you help with the Skylark." His eyes went from his daughter to the messy desk. "Hey, I know how you can help pay."

"How, Dad?" Mary's eyes danced with eagerness as she waited for his answer.

"You can clean off my desk. Put the invoices in numerical order."

"Okay." Mary sighed, dropping onto the chair behind the desk. She'd straightened his messy papers so many times that the job had become boring. "But if you sell some new tires, can I help put them on?" Although Mary's only job was holding the lug nuts, she enjoyed watching. The blasting noise the air impact made reminded Mary of a toot. Each turn of the nut made her giggle.

"What are you smiling about?" her mother asked, bringing Mary from her thoughts.

"Nothing," Mary answered. "You didn't tell me the story."

Her mother began the story Mary had heard well over a dozen times. "I was sixteen—a teenager with a driver's license. I didn't want just any ole car. My dream was to own a muscle car. I wanted a 1970 Chevelle."

"But this is a '72?" Mary interrupted.

"I thought you wanted to hear the story," Eva said. "I'll get to that part." She shook her head and chuckled at her daughter's impatience. "When seeing a Chevelle sitting outside, I went inside Grandpa Kelly's garage to ask if he would sell it. The car had been in an accident. Somebody smashed the grill, hood, and front fender. That's when I met your father."

"You thought Dad was cute, didn't you, Mom?" Mary added impatiently.

"Are you going to tell the story, or do you want me to?" Eva smiled and was about to continue when a black car drove up alongside them. Eva couldn't see inside the tinted windows. "What the heck?"

The passenger-side window opened. A black man with a beard yelled for her to pull over.

"I don't have the time for this," Eva mumbled as she downshifted and stopped close to the curb. The car drove next to her, so close that she checked the mirror to see if they scratched the side. "What do you want?"

"We need you to open the trunk," the man ordered.

"Why? What the hell do you want?" Eva asked.

The bearded man in the passenger's seat pointed a gun at her. "Just give us the drugs."

***

Eva slowly pushed in the clutch and slid the car into gear. Her right foot took the pedal straight down to the floor. The back of Mary's head hit the seat as the Chevelle went from zero to sixty in five seconds. The smoke from the squealing tires covered her escape.

"Hold on, Mary," she whispered from the side of her mouth.

"Mom, why are you driving so fast?" Mary yelled.

"Hold on, Mary," she replied without looking at her. "Just trying to get to school on time." Eva never drove recklessly or fast with Mary in the car, but she feared she was in more danger by the man with the gun. When she checked for the car in the rearview, it wasn't there. *It appears I have lost them. I'll go to the police once Mary's safe at school.* Her face lit up. It had been years since she tested the Chevelle's horsepower and her driving skills. She took the car back to the posted limit and looked at the surroundings. Somewhere in the escape, she had taken a wrong turn.

"That was fun, Mom," Mary said, smiling.

"You think so? Me too," she lied, matching Mary's grin. Her smile faded quickly when the black car came into view. *How did they find me?* She turned right onto the next street then took a quick left at the next intersection, hoping to lose them. It wasn't until she completed the turn that she noticed the dead-end sign. "Crap."

"Aren't you going to finish the story?" Mary asked, interrupting her thoughts. Mary continued the story, unmindful of what was happening. "You didn't like Dad right away but wanted the Chevelle."

"Yes, Mary," Eva said. "Can I finish the story tonight after school?"

The road ended in a parking lot in front of an abandoned factory. Eva made a U-turn and, seeing the black car positioned across both sides of the street, waited at the entrance. *What in the hell do they want? Can't they see I have a child with me?*

"Why is that car parked in the middle of the road?" Mary asked.

"I don't know, Mary. I think they've mistaken me for someone else." She took her hand off the red ball, reached for her purse, then tossed it onto Mary's lap. "Take out my cell phone and dial 911."

"Why?"

"Just do it!" Eva yelled. The only plan she could think of was to stall by outdriving them. It would put Mary's life in danger, but the man had a gun. *Who knows what he'll do if he catches us?* "Put it on speaker."

"Dispatch. How may I direct your call?" a man answered.

"This is Eva Kelly. I'm driving a 1972 Chevelle. I have my daughter in the car with me. I'm on…" She paused, not knowing the name of the street. "I don't know what street I'm on. It's a dead-end street in the parking lot of an abandoned factory," Eva yelled. "I don't know the name," she repeated as a wave of panic hit her. "Two men in black in a Cadillac. They're following me."

"Do you know for sure they are following you?" the dispatcher asked.

"Yes. They have a gun. Oh my God. They're driving straight at us." Eva pushed in the clutch and floored the gas pedal. The tires spun for a few seconds, then when they gripped the uneven pavement, the car shot across the parking lot at top speed. Eva met them head-on, turning sharply at the entrance to avoid a collision.

"Get down!" she screamed at Mary when bullets came through the windshield and hit the top of Mary's seat—just missing her head.

"I'm scared!" Mary cried before sliding down in the seat.

Eva decided the only thing to do was pull up close to the factory, get Mary out of the car undetected, and lead them away. "Take my cell phone." She placed it in her daughter's hand. "When I stop, I want you to jump out of the car. Run as fast as you can and hide. After you find a safe spot, call Dad."

"But I'm scared," Mary repeated. "The man is shooting at us."

"Promise me. You will do what I say."

After Mary's assurance, Eva raced toward the factory and stopped in front. Eva kissed Mary on the forehead. "I love you, Mary. Tell your father that I love him."

As soon as Mary's feet hit the cement, her round eyes met her mothers. "I love you, Mom."

"Go. Hurry, Mary," Eva urged.

"But why can't I stay with you?"

"Run!" Eva screamed before squealing away. Another bullet came through the window, striking her in the left shoulder. She winced but ignored the pain. *At least it wasn't my shifting arm. I can still drive. I have to lead them away from Mary.*

Eva's plan to lead them away was working. Her victory was short-lived, though. As Eva headed toward the only exit out of the factory parking lot, the bearded black man stood in the entrance. With a gun pointed straight at her, Eva had two choices—stop or run him down. Her strict Catholic upbringing had taught her to obey the commandments. The fifth commandment—thou should not kill—was the one she'd thought she would never have to break.

At the last second, Eva slammed on the brakes, stopping inches from him. The car behind hit the brakes and swerved to miss her. The bearded man walked around to the side and tapped on the window. Eva's legs were shaking so severely that her left foot slipped off the clutch, and the engine stalled. She reached for the lever and slowly cranked down the window.

"Who the hell are you?" the man asked. A tattoo of a cobra on his neck peeked out from his half-zipped sweatshirt.

"Eva," she answered, her voice raspy.

"Are you new?"

"No, you idiot. We got the wrong car." The driver of the car came walking up from behind. His height and muscular build intimidated Eva. His platinum hair almost matched his pale skin. Without any warning, he lifted his gun and shot Eva in the chest. As her world went dark, she prayed to God to take care of Mary and her husband.

"Why did you kill her?" the tattooed man asked.

"No witnesses," he grumbled. "Where's the kid?"

"You're not killing a kid," the tattooed man answered.

"I wouldn't have had to kill either of them if you would have gotten the right car," the blond said before kicking the tire.

"Shane said he put the drugs in a '69 Skylark."

The shooter walked to the front and told the tattooed man to follow. He pointed at the emblem in the grill. "This a Chevelle."

"Shane said it was black with gold stripes," the tattooed man said. "It's an honest mistake."

"You don't know anything about cars, do you?" The blond shook his head. "Your lack of knowledge just cost two lives."

"I'm not letting you kill that little girl," the tattooed man repeated before stepping in front of him. "She didn't get a good look at us anyway."

The muscular man pushed him aside, and he walked back to the car. A police siren squealed off in the distance. "Get in," he ordered.

The tattooed man tucked the weapon into his waistband and followed. "The sirens are getting louder." He pointed then looked around one last time before climbing in the passenger side. "Do you think that bitch called the cops?"

"You better hope that girl didn't get a good look at us." The blond gave the tattooed man a threatening glance before starting the car. "I'm not going back to the pen. I just did five years for theft."

The police's sirens sounded only blocks away. The two men didn't know if the police were coming to the factory, but they weren't taking any chances.

"The boss will kill us if she talks," the blond said. He climbed back out of the car and hurried to the passenger side of the Chevelle.

"What are you doing?" the tattooed man yelled. "Come on. They're only a few minutes out."

The blond opened the door, reached into the glove compartment, and read the owner's name and address on the registration. "I want to know her name. I may have to come after the kid and the family," he said.

He hurried to the car and jumped in. The engine roared as he pushed the pedal to the floor. They left unnoticed, escaping detection by only seconds.

"She said her name was Eva," the tattooed man pointed out. "We could've just asked Shane."

"I don't trust Shane. Besides, if I have to kill them, it won't be at the garage." He took the car down to the posted speed limit to avoid suspicion. "We still have to find the Skylark."

Chapter Two

Ten years later

A dim light highlighted a small portion of the room. Mary opened her sleepy eyes briefly then closed them. A scream startled her awake. She sat up quickly and found herself on the couch with the television still on.

"What the hell? I thought I set the timer." She dug out the remote, which had fallen between cushions, and pointed it at the screen. "Damn batteries," she cursed when it didn't work. After striking it several times on her hand, the channel changed. Cowboys and horses filled the screen. "I hate westerns." When the controller wouldn't work again, Mary tossed it on the couch, and it bounced and landed on the floor. She released a frustrated sigh and fell backward. "I guess I'm watching this channel or going to bed."

Going to bed and falling asleep with her mother's murder playing in her mind was out of the question. Tomorrow would be the tenth anniversary of her mother's death. Would it be another wasted trip to the police precinct? It was always the same. They had no new information, and the detectives would have let her know if they had any leads. They wouldn't make any progress if they didn't investigate and hadn't even looked at the case in nine years. If only someone would take the initiative.

After watching for a few minutes, she got interested in the movie's plot. The story was about a man seeking revenge on three men for killing his wife and daughter. Mary had wanted payback for her mother's murder for ten years. She'd often considered taking the matter into her own hands and hiring a private investigator, but she lacked the resources. Working at her father's garage, she barely had the money to pay rent and food. She could move back home to save money, but her father had a new wife and a new family. Mary couldn't bear to watch her father kiss a woman other than her mother. Her dad had always wanted to pass the garage onto a son—not a daughter. *So why can't I move on with my life like he has?*

"If only I could be that brave," Mary whispered when the program got over. With tears in her eyes, Mary reached behind the screen and turned off the power. "I have to get up in four hours." She dragged herself into the bathroom to brush her teeth. "Oh, hell with it. I'll do it in the morning."

She lay awake for hours. Sleep finally took her at six o'clock, then the alarm woke her an hour later. Half-awake, Mary shuffled to the shower.

When she walked into the police station, the dread in the detective's eyes and the eye roll he gave her were enough to make her scream. *Get off your asses and do your job!* But Mary remained silent. *Isn't that what a good Catholic girl is supposed to do?*

Today, a new man sat at the desk across from Detective Skinners. He was young, having barely enough testosterone to be a man. His wavy blond locks reminded Mary of her father when he was young. He stood, straightened his tie, and faced her.

"Any new leads in my mother's case?" she asked him.

"Hi, I'm Detective Ryan." The detective held out his hand, confident Mary would shake it.

Mary gave him a sideways glance. If she hadn't remembered him from high school, she would've thought he had a made-up name to make him sound macho. As she shook his hand, she wondered if he remembered her. *Why would he?*

Gunner Ryan had been popular. He'd been the high school quarterback and would've gone pro if he hadn't blown out his shoulder playing football in college. Mary was a freshman when Gunner was a senior. She'd preferred to stay in the shadows, only had one friend, and had rarely gone to high school games. Mary had spent her Friday nights in karate class. That was where she'd met her only friend, Jasmine.

Gunner's large hand wrapped around hers. When he held it longer than she liked, it brought back her insecurities around men. When he let go, he took a step back to check out her figure. Mary reddened but let his disrespect slide.

"No leads, Mary," Detective Skinner said.

"Is anyone even working on it?" Her voice rose.

"What case are we talking about?" Gunner interrupted.

"It's a cold case. Nothing you need to insert yourself in, Ryan," Skinner warned.

"Cold case?" The volume of Mary's voice elevated further. "You mean to tell me I've been coming in here for ten years, and no one's even investigating it?"

"Calm down, Mary," Skinner said, moving his hands downward. "Until we get more leads, there is nothing we can do."

Balling her hands into fists at her sides, Mary took in a breath to calm her temper. She wanted to punch the detective in the face for lying to her for the past nine years. That was if he'd even given it a fair investigation the first year. She'd given him the benefit of the doubt—something Mary was sure he didn't deserve.

The man was in his fifties now. His brown hair was cut short and graying above his ears. He looked distinguished and seasoned, but Mary considered him to be lazy and stupid. *Probably couldn't solve a case even if the evidence was right in front of him.*

"Do you sleep at night, Detective Skinner?" She didn't wait for him to answer. "I haven't had a good night's sleep since it happened." The movie she'd watched the night before popped into her head. "I should have done this years ago," Mary grumbled on the way out.

"Don't do anything stupid, Mary!" Skinner yelled as she walked away.

Mary stopped at the door and faced Skinner. "I'll leave that to you," Mary flung at him before leaving the precinct, fuming.

The drive to the garage took her half as long as usual. She arrived at the garage at nine thirty. After a trip to the police station, she didn't usually arrive until noon. The morning entailed a trip to the station followed by a drive to the cemetery and to the place where it'd happened.

When Mary walked inside, Agnes, her stepmother, and Josh, her half-brother, were behind the counter. Mary's face showed no expression. She'd perfected hiding her true feelings. "What brings you two here this morning? Does your car need servicing?" she confronted them.

"We thought your father might need help," Agnes said as if she felt the need to defend her presence.

"Won't Josh be late for school?" It was a hint for both of them to leave.

"I'm already late," Josh complained. "Can we go?"

"Will you be all right, dear?" Agnes asked after gathering her belongings.

Mary took in a breath. *Be nice. Keep your cool.* "Yes, sorry I was late," Mary said, faking a smile. She wanted to yell, scream, and complain about the injustice her mother had received. But that would only add to the tension between them. The awkwardness was mostly Mary's fault. At least she recognized it. Agnes always tried to bond with her, but Mary saw Agnes as a replacement for her mother. A betrayal to her mother's memory. Sure, her father had done the honorable thing and waited a year before dating, but Mary thought—as most children did—that her parents had been in love and were meant to be together forever.

"Well, we're off." Agnes headed to the door with Josh in tow.

"See ya later, Josh," Mary said just before the door closed. She had no problem with Josh. She barely knew him. Mary had been fifteen when he was born, and she'd moved out of the house at eighteen.

I will never know who killed my mother. I will never feel safe until I do. Tears ran down her face. When the door opened suddenly, Mary turned away to wipe them on her shirt before checking to see who'd come in.

"I just came back to invite you over for cake and ice cream on Saturday. It's Josh's birthday."

"I'll try," Mary answered.

"I hope you can make it. It will mean a lot to your father—and Josh."

"How old is he?" Mary asked, although she already knew the answer.

"Seven," Agnes answered politely and walked out.

Mary reached inside her purse for a bag of her favorite comfort food. She popped a few into her mouth and closed the bag. As the chocolate melted in her mouth, her anxiety lifted.

Her dad had made improvements to the building over the past four years. Just before Mary graduated from high school, her father had built an addition to the front. The space included a showroom to display and sell tires, a front desk, and a customer waiting area. After her graduation, her father had put her to work selling tires and setting up appointments. There was no college offered as her mother always wanted—only a job. When Agnes had insisted Mary's father start a college fund for Josh, Mary resented her even more.

Mary played with the triquetra symbol hanging from her neck and stared off into space. When the door opened, Mary dropped the necklace. "Good afternoon, sir," she said, her voice ringing out.

An older man hobbled in, holding a cane in one hand for support. "Hello there, young lady," he said with a wide smile.

Mary returned his smile. "Can I help you?"

The man's happy face made Mary realize why she enjoyed the job. The customers were her lifeline to the world. After her mother's death, Mary liked to blend into the background and talk only when necessary—which was hardly ever. Detached was a better way to describe her shyness.

"My old Buick needs a set of tires."

"I can help with that," Mary said as she came out from behind the counter.

"Everyone thinks I should put the ol' gal out to pasture, but I think all she needs is a change of oil and a set of tires."

"Before I sell you tires, can I check the tread and listen to the engine?"

"Why would a good-looking gal like you want to that?" he flirted. "Shouldn't you get a fella?"

"Humor me." Mary giggled. "I'll call man if you're saying you won't give a girl a chance." *Another chauvinist. When will men accept that women can do their jobs just as well?* Mary gave him a wink.

"Sure thing, little lady," he said in a humorous tone, returning her wink. "Thank you," he added when Mary opened the door for him. He hobbled out, shifting his weight onto his right leg. "There was a day when I would've asked an attractive lady like you out to dinner."

With reddened cheeks, Mary tossed her long auburn waves behind herself. "If only you were a few years younger," she said before giggling.

When they reached his car, the man climbed inside.

"Pop the hood." When he released the hood, Mary lifted it. "Start it up." In one try, the engine started. Other than the timing being off slightly, the engine sounded nice. "How many miles do you have on it?"

"Around sixty-five thousand," he answered.

"Are there any other problems?"

"It pulls to the left."

Mary walked around the car to check the tires while the man remained in front. Bad alignment had worn down the tires on the inside. "Looks like your wheels are out of alignment. Does your car pull when you push on the breaks or all the time?"

"More when I'm braking. Does that matter?"

"Yes, it could be only an alignment, but it also could be the brakes, tie rods, or even the ball joints. Perhaps all the above."

"That sounds expensive." The man's brows met in the center. "Maybe I should wait for a fella?"

Mary ignored his sexist remark and tried to sway his decision. "We'll give you wheel alignment and balance for free when you buy four tires. Let's hope that's all that's wrong."

"Need my help?" Shane appeared out of nowhere.

"Finally, someone that knows what's going on," the man complained. "The lady here says I may need new brakes, wheel alignment, and ball joints."

"Possibly," Mary corrected. "Can you help this man, Shane? I'm afraid I may break a nail." Mary rolled her eyes before holding out her hand.

Shane smiled and asked him the same questions and performed the same procedures Mary had. When he bent down to check the tires, Mary saw a tattoo of a snakehead on his chest. Mary only got a glimpse of it, but she recognized it from somewhere. "Mary is right, sir. Your wheels are out of alignment." He smiled at Mary. "I'll check out the rest." Shane climbed in behind the wheel and drove the Buick into the last bay. Vehicles filled the first two.

"Would you like to wait inside? We have a television and comfortable chairs." Mary hurried ahead and opened the door. Several lines were ringing, but she waited for him to hobble inside before running to answer them. "Have a seat," she called before picking up the phone. "Kelly's garage, can you hold please?" The first line was a call for Shane. The second was her stepmother calling to talk to her father, and the third line was for Mary.

"Hi, Mary, this is Detective Ryan."

"Hello, do you have some new evidence or something?"

"I wondered if we could meet somewhere to talk?" Gunner asked instead of answering the question.

"Well, I don't know," she said.

"It's about your mother's case," Gunner answered.

"When?"

"Tonight, at seven. We could meet at the diner a few blocks away from your garage."

"Ah… ah…" Mary was tongue-tied. Gunner Ryan was on the phone. So many girls in high school, including her, would have been ecstatic to hear his voice on the line. *How does Gunner know where I work? He's a cop, dummy.* "I have someplace to be at seven."

"Would eight work out better for you—or tomorrow night, perhaps?"

"See ya at eight," Mary said, hanging up before he confirmed. Mary reached into her bag for the thing that gave her comfort and popped a few M&M's in her mouth. As they did their magic, Mary counted the drawer while the computer ran through its checks. On a typical day, Mary counted the cash drawer first.

As she placed the drawer in the register, Mary's mind drifted back to high school. What would Jasmine think of her going to dinner with Gunner—or even talking to him? Jasmine Jones, whom Mary had nicknamed JJ, was someone she always depended on to have her back, no matter what. JJ had lost a father in a car crash just weeks before the murder. They each knew how much it hurt to lose a parent—their grief bonded their friendship.

Gunner was more handsome than he'd been in high school. She and JJ would giggle when he walked past them in the hall. Mary had fantasized about what it would be like to date the most popular guy at school. Just a look in her direction would've sent her heart pounding.

Jasmine, on the other hand, had been attracted to Gunner's teammate, Tyrone Washington. Jasmine joked that he was flawless, a hunk of chocolate chiseled to perfection. Tyrone stood well over six feet tall. He had rock-hard abs and a smile that made everyone feel welcome. There was a smile on her face as she checked the computer for the correct size of tires.

Shane returned thirty minutes later, saying the man needed new ball joints. Mary hated to tell the man it would be over a thousand dollars, because that was a lot for anyone to pay. After Shane explained that the price included the ball joints, four tires, and labor, the man gave Shane his approval to proceed.

"Maybe I should sell it," the man complained.

"Your car runs great," Mary answered. "How long have you owned it?"

"Ten years."

"You have less than sixty thousand miles on it. You don't drive a lot. And new cars are expensive. Who needs car payments?" Mary said.

"Never thought about it that way." He nodded. "You're a smart young lady, aren't you?"

The garage remained busy until after lunch. Mary hadn't eaten breakfast, and her stomach growled with hunger. When her father came to the showroom and said he was sending Shane for burgers, Mary ordered one with the works. Business never picked up after that for the rest of the day. Mary spent the time cleaning and straightening the showroom. The chrome rims on display sparkled under the showroom lights, attracting prospective buyers.

An hour before closing, her father returned. "I'm so sorry, Mary. I've forgotten what day it was." He wrapped his arm around her and held her for several minutes. "When you were late this morning, I thought maybe you had a doctor's appointment. I forget to write things down sometimes."

"It's okay, Dad. You have a new family to worry about now." Mary pulled away and forced a smile to hide her resentment.

"I loved your mother more than words can express. I miss her, too, Mary."

"I hear Josh is having a birthday party on Saturday," Mary said to change the subject and to stop herself from saying how she felt. *You didn't waste any time moving on with your life.*

"It's hard to believe he'll turn seven already," he answered. "Will you come? Josh would like that." He reached for her hand. "I would like that."

Mary turned away to avoid his touch. Since her father had remarried, his concern seemed phony. Deep down, Mary knew he loved her, but how quickly he'd gotten over her mother was an insult to her memory. "I will try."

"It upsets me to see you all alone."

"I'm not all alone. I have JJ," Mary said.

"You never went to your high school prom." He grabbed her hand. "I've never seen you on a date."

"I'm fine." Mary pushed him away. "This party isn't another setup, is it?"

"No, I thought it would be nice to invite a few friends."

Mary looked at him sideways. "You were planning on fixing me up, weren't you?" When his face reddened, she knew she'd guessed right. "Look, Dad, I have a date tonight after karate class," Mary fibbed.

"Really?" His left eyebrow rose.

"Yes, so will you quit trying to fix me up?"

"Do I know this man?"

Mary wanted to say, "Why would you care?" But the phone rang, giving her a way out of the conversation. She saw the door to the garage close as she answered the phone.

Chapter Three

Gunner was waiting in a booth next to the window. Mary ambled over, still hesitant of the encounter. JJ had laughed when she'd told her about the meeting and asked her to inquire if he and Tyrone were still friends. Mary had said she would only if Gunner brought up the subject.

Every inch of Mary's body shook as he stood to greet her.

"Hi, Mary, thanks for agreeing to meet me." Gunner's words were like fine wine—easy on the palate and leaving her wanting more. His gaze traveled the length of her body before resting on her eyes. "Have a seat." He waited for Mary to sit before doing the same. He smiled. "What have you been doing since high school?"

"Oh, nothing, just working at the garage." She shrugged. "I didn't think you even knew who I was back then."

"How could I not?"

"I didn't think anyone remembered the shooting," Mary answered, avoiding eye contact.

"That wasn't the reason I remember you." Gunner's smile widened. "Almost every guy on the football team wanted to ask you out."

"Even Tyrone?"

"Oh, you had a crush on Tyrone. That explains why I couldn't get your attention," he teased.

"No, I mean, yes," Mary stuttered. "My friend JJ had an awful crush." *Is Gunner saying he was interested in me?* "What is Tyrone doing now?"

"I thought it was your friend who had a crush?" Gunner asked, continuing to tease.

"I'm asking for her?" Mary said.

"Sure." He laughed. "Tyrone is an investment banker. Works at a bank here in the city."

"I'll tell her." Mary blushed. To avoid his stare and calm her nerves, she wrapped her finger around her necklace and looked out the window.

"Can I get either of you something to drink?" a waitress asked as she set two menus on the table.

Mary let go of her chain and let it fall between her breasts. "Iced tea," Mary said after Gunner directed her to go first, then he ordered the same.

"So, the great Gunner Ryan became a cop." Mary smiled when her words sounded sarcastic.

"Yeah, that's what happens when you blow out a shoulder."

"I was sorry to hear that." Mary meant it. "I know what it's like to have to give up your dream."

"Oh, your mother's murder," Gunner said sadly.

"No, it wasn't that. Well, some of it was." Mary looked out the window. It was almost dark. "No money."

"I'm sorry. I know you graduated with honors."

To hear Gunner had even paid attention surprised her. "Me too," Mary said.

The waitress returned with their drinks and asked if they'd decided what to order.

"I'll have a salad. No tomatoes," Mary said.

"Oh, you're one of those girls," Gunner said. "I'll have a cheeseburger and fries."

"I eat. I had a burger for lunch," Mary said.

"A whole burger?" Gunner teased.

"Give me what he's having," Mary ordered to shut him up. "And yes, I still want the salad. With ranch dressing."

"A salad sounds nice. Add that to my order, as well." Gunner gave the waitress a flirty smile. "Put her tomatoes on mine."

Mary wasn't sure if he really wanted a salad or if he'd ordered it to tease her. "Won't your body go into shock?"

"Hey, I like a salad now and then."

"Sure you do." Mary giggled, and Gunner joined her. As soon as the laughter stopped, Mary asked, "So, do you have new information on my mother's case?"

"No, I—"

"Then why the meeting?" Mary interrupted.

"I wanted to tell you that I'll take a look at it in my free time. Sometimes fresh eyes can see evidence in a new way."

"Do you know how many times someone has told me this?" Mary's voice rose as she stood. When Gunner didn't reply, she answered, "Four."

To defuse her temper, Mary sat back down and reached for the sugar packets. She pulled out one regular sugar and one diet, ripped them open, and poured them into her tea. "I like it sweet," Mary said in a friendly tone when she caught him watching her intently. She stirred the tea several times to dissolve the sugar before taking a drink.

"There's been four different detectives." Gunner seemed surprised. "Sorry," he said. "I saw how disappointed you looked this morning and wanted to help."

"The captain or somebody assigned Detective Skinner to my mother's case five years ago," Mary told him. "I don't know if he's even looked at it."

The waitress returned with their salads. "I gave you her tomatoes," she said, setting the plate in front of Gunner. Her smile widened when Gunner thanked her.

The way the woman responded to his personality—and his pearly whites—made Mary wonder if that was how he got women to do what he wanted. His charm had convinced her to accept his invitation to dinner. Gunner didn't have any new information, and deep down inside, she'd realized that.

"Is there a woman in your life?" Mary asked. She'd been dying to know since she saw him at the precinct.

"Why?" he asked, dodging the question.

"How does she feel about you going to dinner with a single woman?" Mary's eyes met his.

"She's not the jealous type." Gunner smirked. When Mary didn't smile at his comment, Gunner added, "Skinner must have read the file, because he mentioned a few details."

"Details?"

The waitress returned with their meals. A piece of lettuce and a pickle were placed next to the burger. "I forgot condiments," she apologized after setting their plates in front of them. The waitress grabbed the ketchup and mustard off the table next to theirs and sat them in front of Gunner. "There you go."

"The car," Gunner said as soon as she left. He squeezed a small amount of ketchup onto his burger and some next to the fries.

"What? No tomato?" Mary teased.

"Tomatoes are for salads only—and tacos."

"My mother's car or the one that chased us?" Mary asked. Her mind drifted to the week before the accident. The impact made the same sound as it had when her dad showed her how to use it. It was the first time. Usually, all he would allow her to do was hand him the lug nuts.

The bottle made a flatulence sound as she squeezed a generous amount of ketchup onto her bun then again as she smothered the fries.

Her faced warmed when she looked up to find Gunner studying her. "What?" Smiling, she applied a small portion of mustard to the bun and pickles. She blushed again. "What?" she repeated before taking a generous bite.

"You must like ketchup." Gunner smiled. When some of the ketchup dripped onto her cheek, he wiped it off with his finger then licked it off.

"Did I get some on my face?" Mary set down the burger and reached for a napkin.

"Why didn't you date anyone in high school?" Gunner probed.

"How do you know I didn't?" Mary looked at him sideways. "Maybe I dated someone at a different school. Perhaps I like girls?"

"Are you a lesbian?" Gunner asked quickly. "It's okay if you are. I... I..." He shrugged. "I'm cool with it." His eyes met Mary's. "Also disappointed."

"Why would that disappoint you?"

"Come on, Mary. Are you that naïve?" Gunner whispered.

Is he hitting on me? He's a married man. His hand rested inches from hers. She pulled it away and straightened in the seat. Her mind went to the Chevelle tucked away in the trailer behind the garage. She hadn't set eyes on it since the murder.

"If you don't mind, I haven't eaten all day."

"Go ahead," Mary said, gesturing toward his meal. Mary copied his actions, remaining silent until her last bite. "You never answered—what car were you asking about?"

"Your mother's. The report indicated the killers might have mistaken her for someone else." Gunner emptied his glass. The ice jiggled as he set it down. "It was a black 1972 Chevelle with gold stripes. Who could misidentify that?"

"Yeah, I wondered the same." Mary looked him in the eye. "Gunner, thanks for caring."

"I wanted to talk to you when I heard about your mother's murder, but I didn't know what to say," Gunner said as he rested his hand over Mary's. "I acted like a self-absorbed jock."

"It's okay," Mary answered. This time, she didn't pull away. "I was in another world back then. Still am."

When Gunner removed his hand, Mary was sure it was to calm what was happening between them. *What is happening? Or am I the only one having trouble breathing? Is his heart beating double time?*

"So, what was so important that you couldn't meet me at seven?" Gunner asked.

"Karate class. I took it up after the murder," Mary admitted, only to sound badass.

"How far did you get?"

"Black belt," she bragged.

"Oh, you're good." Gunner nodded. "I got a lot of training at the academy."

"What kind?" Mary asked. She didn't want to explain that having a black belt was only the first part of the training. Most people thought earning a black belt would make them an expert. Depending on the trainer, though, there could be a lot more to learn. Jasmine had given up after earning a brown belt. Jasmine said she could protect herself if necessary— and that was all she wanted.

"Firearms and self-defense. We had to be in shape physically as well."

"I always wanted to know how to shoot a gun," Mary let slip. *Please don't ask me why. I don't want to admit that I want to hunt down my mother's killers.*

"Why? When would you have the need?" Gunner asked.

Crap! Think of something, Mary. "It was just after the shooting. I didn't feel safe." Mary sighed. A half-truth was better than a lie. *At least he won't think I'm crazy.*

"That's understandable," Gunner said. "Don't you have a boyfriend to make you feel safe?"

"Are you saying I need a man to protect me?" Mary took offense.

"No, but maybe someone would enjoy it if given a chance," Gunner answered in a deflected tone. "Sorry. I didn't come to argue."

"Why did you ask me here?" Mary eyed him with skepticism.

"I told you. I want to take another look at your mother's case."

"You don't need my permission for that." Mary pulled a twenty from her purse, tossed it on the table, then stood. "Nice seeing you again, Gunner." Mary left him sitting in the booth and headed toward the exit.

"Mary, please!" Gunner called. "You're overreacting." Gunner retrieved money from his wallet and tossed it onto the table. "Wait!" he yelled as she left the diner. He hurried to stop her, catching up with her outside her car. "What are you afraid of?"

Mary removed her hand from the door handle, rolled her eyes, and turned to face him. "I'm sorry, Gunner. You were just trying to be nice. I have to go."

With a click of the remote, the locks opened, and she climbed in. Gunner stood at the window. It was a hot July night, and he was in a casual T-shirt and jeans. He looked more like the boy she remembered from high school than the grown-up stuffed shirt she'd met that morning. Mary rolled down the window and looked up at him. "Have a nice life, Gunner. It was nice to see you again."

"Don't leave, Mary." Gunner placed his hand on the door.

"Let me know if you turn up anything," Mary said before backing away. When she looked in the rearview, Gunner was still standing where she'd left him.

***

Gunner's childhood home was enormous for a family of four. It was just him and his mother in the two-story house. His father had died, and his big sister, Laura, was married with two children. The place was dark except for the room at the back of the house. His mother must still be awake. With a glance at his phone, he saw it was nearly midnight. Hopefully, she only left the light on and wasn't waiting up for him.

Gunner missed his freedom. He'd grown accustomed to living on his own. Straight out of high school, he'd stayed in a fraternity house with five other guys. He hadn't been alone in the place, but he'd had a room of his own. There weren't parents telling him what time to get up or what time to be home. His fraternity had thrown parties almost every weekend, but most of the time, Gunner had stayed clear. Going to school for law enforcement had meant drugs and alcohol were grounds for expulsion. Gunner had only broken that rule twice—once for his twenty-first birthday and when his father died.

A drunk driver had run a red light and T-boned his father's car, killing him instantly. After the tragic traffic accident, Gunner had almost quit school because of his trouble coping with his grief. That was when he'd moved back home. Together, he and his mother had worked through a difficult time, and he didn't want her to live alone. If only Mary would have let him tell her—he understood what it was like to lose a parent. If someone had killed his mother, he would have done just about anything to bring the killers to justice. In a sense, he'd done that with his father.

When Mary walked into the precinct that morning, his heart had gone out to her. Gunner had been attracted to Mary in high school, but she'd been forbidden fruit. As a freshman, she was too young for a senior. Having sex with her would have been a way for an eighteen-year-old boy to get arrested. And he wanted that and much more. How could he stay away from her now that he'd seen what a beautiful woman she'd become?

"You shouldn't wait up for me, Mom," Gunner said when he entered the kitchen. His mother was sitting at the kitchen table. An emptied wineglass and a phone sat in front of her.

"I couldn't sleep until I knew you were all right." His mother yawned, and she smiled when their eyes met.

"I wasn't at work."

"Were you with Tyrone?" She got up from her chair and headed to the sink. "Maybe he could help you meet a girl instead of hanging out with your mother in your spare time." Mrs. Ryan rinsed out the glass and set it on the counter. "I think I'll go to bed." She yawned again.

"I was on a date," Gunner lied, because he knew nothing would make her happier.

"Anyone I know?" She seemed to wake instantly.

"No. I'll let you know if we get serious. Until then, it was just a date," Gunner fibbed to stop her from meddling. His job gave her so many concerns. A woman in his life would soothe her worries. He saw how grandchildren lifted her spirits when his sister visited. If only he had the time to date. His job took up most of his time—time he could be spending with a woman. His loneliness had been easy to ignore until the meeting with Mary. Touching her had made him realize how long it'd been since he'd felt a woman beneath him. Mary's strict catholic upbringing would stop her from climbing into his bed after one passionate embrace. Was he ready for commitment?

The keys made a scratching sound as he tossed them in the silver tray in the hallway. He'd seen his father do the same thing every night when he got home from work. His father was an important man—the city's mayor. Before his death, he was considering a run for governor.

"Good night, Mom," Gunner said, seeing his mother at the top of the steps. He'd been thinking of Mary and hadn't realized she walked past him in the hall.

"Whoever the girl is, she's got you under her spell," she teased. "Good night."

"Good night, Mother," he repeated.

***

Mary's mind went from the meeting with Gunner, to the Chevelle, then to her mother's murder. The whole dinner seemed weird. *Why would my mother's murder interest him?*

He'd barely noticed her at high school, and tonight, he'd acted as if they were friends. The more she thought about the Chevelle, the more she wanted to see it. She hadn't looked at it since that day. The car should have been hers when she turned twenty-one. Her twenty-second birthday had passed months ago, though. The keys for the trailer holding the Chevelle were in the top drawer in her father's desk. She'd seen them while searching for a missing invoice. *If I could sit in it, maybe I would remember something more than I told the police. I was only twelve. There could be lots of details I've missed.*

The garage was dark when she pulled into the lot. Mary drove to the back, parking between the two cars reserved for customers to use while their cars were under repair. The clock radio showed 11:45 p.m. She took out her cell phone, turned on the flashlight, and walked to the alarm to put in the code. No one had activated it. She hurried to the door, and it opened with a push. *Good thing I decided to come. Dad must've forgotten to lock up.*

Tiptoeing to the showroom, she gave the door that separated the customer area from the garage a shake. It was secure. *The safe! Someone could have robbed us.*

Mary ran to the office and tried the knob. The door popped open. She hurried to the safe and put in the combination.

"Thank God," Mary said when she found the money untouched. She shut the safe and gave the dial a spin. *Boy, Dad really must have been in a hurry. I wonder if something happened at home.* Mary retrieved the keys for the trailer and the Chevelle from the desk, planning to call him after doing what she'd come to do.

Her father secured the trailer's side door with a padlock. Mary found two keys on the ring and tried the smallest one. With one turn, the padlock opened. She left the lock hanging on the clasp and used the second key to open the door. She pointed the flashlight from her phone at the car. There had to be at least an inch of dust on it. Mary ran her hand across the dirty hood, revealing the golden stripes.

Like a flash of lightning, she was twelve again, sitting in the car with her mother at her side.

"Hold on, Mary," her mother said before her head slammed back against the seat. The powerful engine vibrated, making the golden strips blur. The vision made Mary lightheaded. She grabbed the side of the car for support.

The bullet holes in the windshield caught her attention. With another flash, she was back in the passenger seat next to her mother. "Run, hide, Mary," her mother called out to her.

Her mother's dried blood had left a dark stain on the seat's leather. Tears ran down her face as the morning of the shooting played in her head. The images and pain were still fresh.

Voices from outside the trailer snapped her from the nightmare. "Mary, they are here—Run!" a voice warned.

With the light of her phone, she scanned the trailer and found no one. Male voices from outside became louder as they got closer to the trailer. Without making a sound, Mary crept to the door and peeked out. It was dark, and she couldn't make out their faces. She recognized one of the voices as Shane's. Mary relaxed and released a sigh. She opened her mouth to make her presence known but remained quiet when Shane spoke.

"They keep the car in here. They probably wouldn't notice it's gone. No one's opened the trailer in years."

"Do you have the keys?" the other man asked. "I could just shoot the lock."

"Gunfire will alert the neighborhood," Shane warned. "I left the alarm off after the old man left. We can just go inside and get them."

"I'll wait here. You go. I'll whistle if anyone shows," the man urged.

When it became quiet again, Mary peeked outside. The man stuck his gun in his waistband and leaned against her car. If Shane saw it, he would know she was there. Her heart pounded. *What will Shane do if he finds me? Why would he steal the Chevelle? Maybe I should just go outside and kick his ass and find out?*

Angrier than scared, Mary stepped toward the door. She paused when remembering the man outdoors had a gun. *I am fast but not quicker than a bullet.* After a deep breath, she dialed Gunner's number. "Come on, come on," she whispered when he didn't pick up until the fourth ring.

"Hello. Who is this?" Gunner answered sleepily.

"Gunner, it's Mary," she whispered.

"Mary, are you all right? Why are you whispering?"

"I need help. I'm in a trailer at the garage," Mary whispered. She hung up and turned off the ringer. Then she hurried to the Chevelle and climbed through the broken window. Trapped with no place to run, her heart pounded as panic took over her mind. *I stand a better chance if I fight.*

"The keys are gone," Shane said. "I searched everywhere."

"Let's just shoot out the lock," the other man urged.

Their voices were right outside the trailer. Mary's mind wrestled with whether she should get out and fight or stay hidden and hope they didn't search the car.

"Look, it's unlocked." The other man held up the padlock and smiled.

"What the hell?" Shane grabbed the lock and opened the door. After a glance inside, Shane opened it as far as the hinges would allow. Just as Mary had earlier, he used his cell as a flashlight to scan the inside. "Someone's been inside here recently."

"How can you tell?"

"Someone's touched the door." He pointed the flashlight on the door where Mary lay just inches away. "There's no dust."

"Could it be the owner?"

Shane shook his head. "I haven't seen him go in here in years."

"Could the girl be snooping around? She's always going to the cops and asking them to reopen the case. If Draco would've killed her, too, we wouldn't have anything to worry about."

"No!" Shane yelled. "The girl's not to be touched."

"Why do you care what happens to the little bitch?"

"She's off-limits." Shane's word sounded final.

"This car is the key to figuring out the whole thing," the gunman said.

Shane turned off the flashlight, halting his search. Lights flashed across the front of the building. "Someone's here," Shane whispered before padlocking the door. "Let's come back another night."

Safe for the moment, Mary released the breath she'd been holding the entire time. *Is Shane behind Mother's murder? But he's been nice to Dad and me.* Her father couldn't function for months after the murder, and Shane had picked up the slack at the garage. *How in the hell will I get out of here without Shane finding out?* Mary climbed out of the car's window. "Hopefully, Gunner's on the way."

When she checked her phone, she saw he'd called her six times. She redialed him.

"Mary, where the hell are you?" His excited voice came on the line. "I've called you several times."

"I'm locked in a trailer behind the garage."

"The big white one?"

"Yes—wait. How do you know it's white?" Mary asked.

"Because I'm staring at it right now."

"Be careful. There's a man with a gun."

"No one's here," Gunner replied.

The doorknob rattled, and the padlock hit the door. "Is that you, Gunner?"

"Yes, where's the key?"

"In my pocket." Mary walked to the door. "Someone locked me inside." Could she trust Gunner with what she'd just heard moments ago? "They didn't know I was in here." *It won't work, Mary. You already warned Gunner about the gun.*

A single gunshot came from the rear of the trailer. Then the whole back end fell to the ground. Gunner stood at the bottom of the ramp. "I shot open the lock," he said, as if saving her was easy. "Are you okay?"

He was dressed in the same clothes he'd worn at the diner. Only, his blond locks were messy, and his green eyes darker.

Mary ran into his arms. "I was so scared," she whispered. Tears ran down her face as his arms wrapped around hers. Gunner held her without speaking for several minutes. When she stepped away, he wiped away the tears. "Thank you for coming, Gunner. I didn't know who else to call."

"Why were you in a trailer in the middle of the night?" Gunner's brows met in the center. "Shouldn't you be in bed?"

"I had an urge to see the Chevelle." She glanced at the trailer. "We talked about it at dinner."

"Don't you think it could wait till the morning?" He smiled as he looked down at her. He pulled her back into his arms without waiting for an answer. "You're shaking."

Mary pushed him away, even though being in Gunner's arms felt safe and warm. To avoid telling him the whole story and what she overheard, Mary simply told him someone had forgotten to set the alarm and left the door unlocked. "It's completely off character for my father to make such a mistake."

"Come, let's talk in my car." Gunner pushed up the ramp and latched it in place without locking it. "It should be safe until tomorrow, but you might want to purchase a new lock."

Mary's heart skipped a beat when Gunner's hand guided her across the parking lot. Like a gentleman, he opened the door for her. When she saw that he drove a four-door sedan, Mary became a little disappointed. With all his sexiness, Mary had pictured him driving a muscle car. A '67 Mustang Fastback or a new Dodge Hellcat with comfy leather seats.

"From the information you gave me, I think it was an inside job?" Gunner said as soon as he got behind the wheel.

"Can we go for a drive? I don't feel safe here," Mary said when all he wanted to do was keep it businesslike. *Isn't that what you wanted, Mary?*

"Sure." Gunner reached into his front pocket, pulled out keys, and put them into the ignition. "Can I drive you home or to your father's house?"

"No, just drive."

They drove around town without speaking. "Turn down here," Mary said, instead of avoiding the place she hadn't visited once a year.

"It's a dead end."

"Yes, I know." They came to the parking lot where Mary had lost her mother forever. "This is where it happened."

Gunner stopped in the center. The full moon illuminated the entire lot and the front of the factory. "Why would your mother come here? It's a dead end. Surely she must have known..." He broke off when he saw Mary's tears. "I'm sorry."

"She drove fast. Very fast. I was frightened." Mary cried.

"I'm sure you were. Anyone would've been. Especially a child." Gunner placed his hand over hers. "But you lived. You were brave, Mary."

"I wasn't brave. I hid in the factory while the two men with snake tattoos killed my mother!" Mary yelled before covering her face with her hand. Her body shook as she cried.

"Did you say snake tattoos?" Gunner raised an eyebrow. "That information wasn't in the file."

"What?" Mary paused and wiped away her tears. "I'm sure I told the police about that."

"Nope. I read the entire file before meeting with you tonight. The statement you gave said nothing about tattoos. You said one man was dark complected and one was Caucasian. You said the white man shot your mother."

"I only said that because I saw a snake tattoo on Shane's neck." Trying to justify her answer, Mary had revealed she knew more.

"What else happened tonight?" Gunner asked. He turned toward her and eyed her with suspicion. "Why were you so frightened?"

"I told you. I thought someone broke into the garage." Mary lowered her lashes as her mind wrestled with telling Gunner. *I did trust him enough to call. And he came.* After releasing a breath, Mary told him his suspicions about an inside job were correct. "Shane was one of the guys at the garage tonight. He's worked for us for ten years. I can't believe he would wait until now to steal... from us." *I almost said Chevelle.*

"Look, I can't arrest them unless something is missing. Otherwise, Shane could just say he had forgotten something and came back to get it."

"I'll check in the morning. I don't know if Shane set the alarm, so will you take me there to check?"

"Sure." Gunner eyed her. "Do you want me to sleep outside your apartment tonight?"

"Would you do that?" Her eyes met his.

"Yes, if it would make you feel safer."

"Would you sleep with me?"

"What?"

"I mean, in my apartment. No, I mean on the couch." She shook her head. "Never mind." Mary turned away out of embarrassment.

"Is it comfortable?" Gunner teased.

"Very. I fall asleep on it all the time." Mary rolled her eyes.

When they drove to the garage, they found Shane had locked the outside door but hadn't activated the alarm. Mary reset it and climbed back into Gunner's car.

"How often do you have to stay on a girl's couch?" Mary asked as they pulled into her apartment complex.

"Every other week," Gunner answered.

"You must get a sore back." Mary giggled.

"When did you move in here?" Gunner asked as she unlocked the door.

Mary flipped on the lights, waited for Gunner, then locked the door. "About five years ago. As soon as I graduated high school."

"It's hard living on your own. Does working at the garage pay well?"

Gunner was making small talk. Mary could see he was nervous about staying. "Have a seat. I'll get some blankets."

When she returned carrying a stack of bedsheets and a blanket, Gunner was sitting on the couch, his feet bare. She wondered what he looked like without his clothes. The tight T-shirt left not much for the imagination. His bulging pectorals and muscular chest were pushing the shirt to the limit. Mary guessed he had washboard abs.

"Sorry." He wiggled his toes. "I didn't take the time to put on socks. When you called, I rushed out of the house."

"That's okay. As you can see, it's casual around here."

An oversized puffy couch sat in the middle with oak tables at each end. Lamps shaped like pineapples rested on top. "When my dad got remarried, he gave me all this furniture, except the couch. I bought that all by myself," Mary bragged.

"It's comfy," Gunner said with a bounce. He jumped to his feet. "Let me help." Gunner grabbed one end of the sheet, and Mary took the other. She slipped a clean case on a pillow and tossed it on the couch. "Will one blanket be enough?" She held out a patchwork quilt reserved only for guests.

"That will be fine." Gunner smiled. "Did you make that?"

"Yes. I live a boring life." Mary sighed. "I go to work then come home."

"Me too," Gunner said.

"But what about your wife?" Mary handed him the quilt, and his hand covered hers.

"I'm not married," Gunner whispered as he looked into her eyes.

"But you said—"

"You asked if the woman in my life knew I was having dinner with a beautiful woman," Gunner interrupted.

"I said single, not beautiful." Mary's eyes locked with his. "You think I'm beautiful?"

"Yes," he said. When his mouth covered hers, Mary let the blanket drop to the floor. Gunner's arms wrapped around her, and he kissed her until they were both out of breath. "I've wanted to do that since the first time I saw you."

"You didn't know I even existed. Jasmine and I talked about how sexy you were." Mary blushed.

"When I saw you for the first time, you were standing in front of the gymnasium. You had on a pink dress that made you look like an angel. Your hair was still wet from the shower you took after gym class." Gunner kissed her on the forehead and placed his hand below her chin, making her look him in the eyes. "You turned me on then. And you're turning me on now."

"How could you remember what I was wearing?" Mary asked. Gunner's mouth returned to hers. He inserted his tongue to deepen the kiss, sending excitement to her loins. Gunner's warm hands roamed under her blouse and found her breasts. She moaned when his mouth left hers to kiss her neck.

"I want you," Gunner whispered.

"I want you too," Mary said.

Gunner picked her up and carried her down the hall.

"Go left," Mary whispered between kisses. They stumbled backward and fell onto the bed. Gunner pulled off his shirt and tossed it on the floor. In just a few minutes, Gunner Ryan would make love to her. She'd fantasized about this so many times at high school that it seemed real. *But this is real.*

Mary undressed to her undergarments. When she looked at Gunner, he was fully nude. His body wrapped around her. His hardness poked her belly. *Am I ready for this?*

With a flick of his fingers, Gunner unfastened her bra. Her breasts bounced free until his hands cupped them.

"This is better than I imagined," Gunner said before taking her breast in his mouth. He kissed the other, teasing them both with his tongue until her nipples hardened.

Does Gunner know he'll be my first? Should I tell him or ask him to stop? The heat from his lips impeded her doubts. Every kiss and every touch sent her body into bliss. Gunner whispered something before taking her—each thrust brought pain between her thighs. When the hurt turned to an ache to be satisfied, Mary moved her hips in time with his. Gunner recognized her signals or had the experience and moved with skill. When Mary screamed with pleasure, Gunner thrust himself inside her, moaned loudly, then released his seed inside her.

"It's been a long time," Gunner said breathlessly. He kissed her on the neck then rolled off her. "Sorry, I got a little carried away."

"Me too," Mary said, only to sound as if she had the experience. She worried what Gunner would say if she told him she was a virgin.

Gunner wrapped his arm and leg around her and pulled her in close. With the warmth of his body touching her back, Mary sank into him and fell asleep.

When the sun filled the room the next morning, Gunner was gone.

"At least I don't have to face him." She yawned. It would have been awkward if he'd stayed, but Mary concluded that she wasn't just another one of his conquests. When peeling back the covers, Mary saw their lovemaking had stained the sheets with her blood and the seed of Gunner's pleasure. *He didn't use a condom.* Panic set in. *Can a woman get pregnant the first time?* She ran into the bathroom to take a shower. *What will Dad say?* He'd raised her to wait until after marriage. The spray hid her tears, and the water washed them away. In Gunner's arms, she was a woman, and now she may have to pay for the pleasure. *At least I don't feel numb anymore.*

After dressing, Mary took the soiled sheets from the bed and stuffed them into the hamper. Then she removed the sheets from the couch that Gunner never used and made the bed. It was Saturday, and tonight, her father expected her to attend a birthday party. If she didn't at least make an appearance, her stepmother would take it personally.

"Stepmother," Mary said out loud. "What would Mom think of Dad's new wife?" Her mother was supposed to be the woman of his dreams—his soul mate.

On the way into the kitchen, Mary found a note from Gunner on the kitchen table. He explained why he had to leave. Gunner didn't want to wake her and had to leave early to go home and change for work. He'd signed the letter "Always Gunner." Not "Love Gunner" or "I want to see you again" but "Always Gunner." *What does that mean?*

After a quick bowl of cereal, Mary gave Jasmin a call to ask if she could catch a ride to the garage to pick up her car. Saturdays were the busiest day of the week for beauticians, but Jasmine only worked until two o'clock and took Sundays off. Jasmine agreed to take her if she told her the details of her date with Gunner. It hadn't been a date, but Mary wasn't in the mood to argue.

The apartment needed a good cleaning. So after taking the sheets to the laundry room in the building, Mary spent the day cleaning. She found that keeping busy kept her mind off the reckless night of passion. A knock at the door shook Mary from her head. She folded the last sheet and hurried to answer.

"Come in." Mary motioned Jasmine inside. "You look beautiful, as always." Mary smiled. Not a hair was out of place. Jasmine's skin was as smooth as silk, and the makeup applied to her eyes made them appear rounder. Mary hadn't even run a comb through her hair after her shower or put on any makeup.

"You look like hell," Jasmine pointed out. "Can I at least fix your hair?" Jasmine hurried to the bathroom and returned moments later with a comb, a spray bottle, a big round brush, and a blow-dryer. "Was your date with Gunner that bad?" After wetting Mary's hair, Jasmine combed out the snarls and dried it with the brush. When she was through, Mary's hair was poufy and shiny.

"That's better." Jasmine smiled. "Now, tell me about the date while I put on your makeup."

"How many times do I have to say it wasn't a date?" Mary asked.

Mary told her they had a lovely meal and reminisced about old times—and that she'd found out Tyrone was an investment banker in the city.

"What old times?" Jasmine asked. "Gunner never talked to either of us."

"We mostly talked about my mother's case. As I said, it wasn't a date."

"Is he still handsome, or did he lose his hair and get fat?" Jasmine giggled.

Mary smiled. "Oh, he's still handsome."

"Hold still while I put on your mascara." Jasmine put the mascara in her bag and handed Mary a compact mirror. "Eat your heart out, Gunner Ryan."

A knock at the door caused them both to jump.

"Are you expecting someone?"

"No, It's probably my neighbor. She stops by now and then to borrow laundry soap or sugar for her coffee." Mary handed Jasmine the compact and walked to the door. "Gunner," Mary exclaimed.

"I thought maybe you could use a ride to the garage to pick up your car," he said as he stepped past her and walked inside. "Oh, hello." Gunner seemed surprised by Jasmine. "Am I interrupting?"

"No, I just stopped to say hi." Jasmine giggled. "I have somewhere to be." She tossed the compact into her purse and hurried to the door.

"JJ, wait," Mary called.

"Call me," Jasmine whispered. She gave Mary a wink and closed the door behind her.

"I have a feeling I've interrupted something," Gunner said.

"She was supposed to give me a ride to pick up my car."

"You look beautiful," Gunner whispered. He pulled her into his arms and placed a long passionate kiss on her lips. "I wanted to do that this morning but didn't want to wake you." The kiss smeared her lipstick and transferred onto Gunner's lips. Before Mary could wipe away the lipstick, Gunner's mouth covered hers again. "I only have an hour," he said breathlessly.

"It won't take that long." Mary grabbed his hand and led him to her bed. They undressed and were on top of it within seconds. Gunner slowed down only long enough to take a condom from his wallet. There was no foreplay—only sex. Gunner slid inside her, and together, they reached their pleasures in seconds. They lay beside each other, breathing heavily.

"Gunner," Mary whispered. "Do you have a girlfriend?"

He rolled onto his side and played with her nipples. They hardened at his touch. "I hope so," he said before leaning down and sucking them.

Mary's loins ached and begged to be satisfied. "Gunner," she whispered.

"Hearing you say my name turns me on."

"Gunner," Mary whispered.

"Oh, hell." Gunner moaned before pulling her on top of him. "Make love to me again."

His forwardness made Mary blush. She gasped when Gunner inserted his penis inside her. Mary had seen a sex scene in an R-rated movie once where the woman took charge. She copied the women's actions. Gunner cupped her breasts as they bounced in front of him. Mary felt a desire to go faster and faster until she screamed in ecstasy. Gunner sounded like he was in pain. He pushed Mary off him, and his seed spilled over the blanket. "Sorry for the mess, Mary. Man, you turn me on."

"Did you have on a condom last night?" Mary asked.

"No, I'm sorry. I wasn't… I didn't plan to sleep with you."

"You planned this," Mary accused. She leaped from out of bed and began to dress.

"No," he argued.

"You had one today," Mary flung at him. She dressed in a hurry and left the bedroom.

Gunner dressed and followed.

"Okay. I stopped at the store and bought some. I put one in my wallet in case it happened again, but I didn't plan it." Gunner walked toward her and forced her to look at him by placing a hand under her chin. "I know you're not that kind of a girl."

"What? A whore?"

"Your parents raised a nice catholic girl," Gunner tried to explain. "I saw the blood on the sheets. I felt you stiffen beneath me."

"And you kept going," Mary cried.

"I was going to stop until I felt you come alive. Then I couldn't."

"So, it's okay to sleep with a virgin if she likes it?" Mary fumed.

Gunner smiled. "Every man wants a virgin, Mary."

"You think this is funny?"

"No, I was laughing at our teachings. The Virgin Mary," Gunner explained.

"Well, let's hope this virgin Mary doesn't get pregnant." Mary's voice escalated. Mary stormed from the room and hurried to the closet by the door. She was tying her shoes when Gunner joined her, fully dressed.

"If that happens, Mary, I will do the right thing," Gunner said, sounding honorable. "I'm late, but I can still take you to get your car," he added when Mary didn't reply.

The ride was awkward and quiet until Gunner turned on the radio. He fiddled with the stations until he stopped at a country station. After the second twangy song, Mary couldn't help herself. "I pictured you as a rock-and-roll kind of guy."

"Habit. It's all Skinner likes. I would rather if you don't mind." When Mary nodded, he put on an easy-listening station. "Better?"

"Thank you. If I had to listen to one more you-did-me-wrong song, I might've jumped out of the car."

"Country isn't that bad," Gunner said. "Oh my God, Skinner has gotten to me."

They both chuckled.

"You're so beautiful when you laugh," Gunner said.

"What? I'm ugly the rest of the time?" Mary teased.

"No, I-I—" Gunner stuttered.

"I'm just yanking your chain."

They laughed again.

The garage was closed when they pulled in. Mary's car was where she'd left it. However, one of the loaner cars was gone. That meant Shane and her father knew she'd returned. It surprised her that he hadn't called to check on her. She pulled her cell from her purse. It was dead. "My phone must have gone dead in the night."

"Do you have a charger in your car?" Gunner asked as he pulled up behind the two vehicles. "Which one's yours?"

"The silver one," Mary joked. Both cars were silver. Hers was a Chevy. "Mine's on the right." Mary's attention went to the trailer. "Before you go, can we check out the trailer? I just want to make sure no one has stolen the Chevelle."

"Sure." Gunner nodded. He put the car in park, turned off the ignition, and followed Mary. "Let me," he urged when Mary had trouble with the rear door.

The dusty car inside brought a smile to Mary's face. "One of these day's I'm going to have to learn to drive it." She looked at Gunner, who looked confused. "Stick shift."

"Oh, I drove one once. I stalled it a lot," Gunner admitted. "Perhaps your father could teach you."

"He's got a new family. He doesn't have time for me." Mary sighed.

"I'm sure he would if you ask," Gunner said. "Can I take a closer look?"

They climbed inside. The sunlight illuminated the front of the car. Gunner gestured to the bullet holes in the windshield and the shattered passenger window. "I know a reputable auto body garage if you want to fix it."

"Would they be open now?"

"I don't know, why?" Gunner gave her a confused expression.

"I don't want to leave it here one more day," Mary explained. "If Shane tried to steal it once, he will try again."

Chapter Four

It'd been a busy day. After Gunner left, she'd used the garage's tow truck to take the Chevelle to the auto body shop Gunner recommended.

When returning to the garage, Mary had parked the tow truck in the exact spot so her father and Shane wouldn't notice someone had used it. She was getting into her car when Shane arrived.

"Did you notice the trailer's missing?" Shane asked.

"Oh my God, has someone stolen it?" Mary pretended to be shocked. "When did you see it last?"

"Last night?"

"When? At closing? Or did you stop back later?" Mary asked to see if he would lie.

Shane looked at her sideways. "I forgot something. When I saw the padlock wasn't closed, I locked it."

"Oh, maybe Dad." Mary smiled to cover the disdain she felt for him. All the years she'd given him credit for helping the family, and it was only a deception. He had something to do with her mother's death, and she was determined to find out what. Until then, Mary planned to play along. "I'll be seeing him later. I'll ask." Mary pasted on a smile.

"Oh, are you going to Josh's party?"

"Yes, I'm on my way to the store now to buy a gift... so gotta go, or I'll be late. See you Monday."

"I'll see you at the party. Your dad invited me too." He smiled proudly.

Mary wanted to call out—*Murderer! Thief! You ruined my family!* —but held in her emotions. "See ya there."

As soon as Mary turned, she relaxed her smile. Her face hurt from pretending. It was going to be hard to work with him now that she knew he had something to do with her mother's death. "Nobody kills my mother and tries to steal her car," Mary grumbled under her breath.

Mary arrived at Josh's party thirty minutes late. Cars lined the street, so Mary parked around the block. The walk gave her time to collect her thoughts.

"You made it!" Her father's voice carried across the room. He left his wife and another couple to greet Mary at the door.

Her body trembled as she scanned the room. Most of the guests were from Agnes's side of the family. A smile returned to Mary's face when she saw her grandparents from her mother's side. She always liked them. They were like second parents to Mary when her mother died. Until her dad remarried. "Hi, Dad." He hugged her. "Sorry I'm late."

"I'm just happy you came," he said, pulling away.

"Joe, will you come here?" Agnes called.

"We ate already, but it was buffet style. Go in the kitchen and help yourself," her father said before leaving her at the door.

"Run when your wife calls," Mary said under her breath. She walked immediately to the couch, where her grandparents sat, looking as uncomfortable as she felt. "Grandma and Grandpa Mulligan, glad to see you." Mary hugged them both.

"We haven't seen you in a month. What have you been up to?" her grandpa asked.

I've had a busy week. I lost my virginity, stole my mother's car, and found out who caused your daughter's death. "I've been busy. I'll visit next week. I promise."

"I'll make beef stew. Your favorite."

"Someday, Grams, you're going to have to show me how you make it. Mine is good, but yours has way more flavor."

"It's because I make it with love, dear." Her smile widened.

"No wonder." Mary giggled. "Excuse me. I'm going to fetch some food before Agnes puts it away. I haven't eaten all day."

There wasn't an open spot on the island counter. Platters of cold cuts, cheeses, vegetables, and fruit covered the top. Mary had expected something warm, but she grabbed a slice of bread and prepared a sandwich. In the center of the table was Josh's birthday cake. It was a full sheet, covered with buttercream frosting and decorated with cars. Mary's mouth watered. She couldn't remember the last time she'd had a piece of cake.

"Thanks for coming, Shane," Mary heard her father say. Her heart sped up, and her blood pressure rose. *Will he bring up the Chevelle?* If she didn't act worried and upset, her father would figure out who'd taken it. Her stomach turned. Mary tossed her half-eaten sandwich into the garbage and started for the back door. Dirty dishes covered the counters and filled the sink. Mary began to clean to avoid Shane and questions about why she'd left before the cake. She rinsed all the plates, stacked them next to the sink, then washed off the countertops. "Great," Mary said under her breath when seeing the dishwasher. Mary loaded the dishes and closed the door. "Agnes would have a dishwasher. Mom had to wash them by hand."

"What did you say, Mary?" Agnes stood behind her.

I hope she didn't hear that. "I said I'm glad you have a dishwasher."

"Oh, I don't expect you to clean up after me," Agnes returned.

"Just trying to help."

"Are you staying for the cake? We're going to sing 'Happy Birthday' in a few minutes." Agnes looked around. "Have you seen Josh anywhere?"

Mary shook her head instead of answering. "Where's Dad?" she asked to escape a conversation with her stepmother. She had to tell him the trailer was missing before Shane did.

"He just went out of the garage to get Josh's present. We had to hide it out there. He's such a sneak." Agnes chuckled.

"Okay, thanks." Fleeing out the back door, Mary headed to the garage. *It's good no one will be around. He'll get upset when I tell him.* The side door was open, so Mary went in. Her father was pushing a red BMX bike. There was a big blue bow on the front and a ribbon wrapped around the handlebars.

"Do you think Josh will like it?" Joe asked.

"Yes, I liked the one you and Mom bought me when I turned twelve."

"Oh, do you think it's too big for him?"

"No, he'll love it." Mary cleared her throat. "Dad, I have something to tell you."

He stopped pushing the bike and stared at her. "Shane told me."

"And you're not upset?" Mary's voice rose.

"Yes, I'll call the police tonight after our company leaves." His face showed no emotion. The tone he'd used made Mary think he didn't care.

"But it was Mom's car."

"Well, Mary, you never seemed interested in driving it. I was thinking about giving it to Josh when he was old enough," he said.

"Josh? Mom wanted me to have it!" Mary yelled. "Tell Josh happy birthday. I can't stay for the cake." Mary stormed out of the garage. As she rounded the corner, her father yelled for her to come back. With her temper boiling, Mary ran to her car. Tears poured after climbing behind the wheel. Her hands shook. "I've had enough. He will never find the car now. I'm going to fix it, paint it, and hide the car somewhere they will never find it."

***

A week passed before Gunner saw Mary again. *Where will I find the time to investigate her mother's case when I'm pulling doubles?* The captain had scheduled him to five on the day he'd last seen Mary—the afternoon they'd made love on his lunch break. A murder case had come in at four thirty, and he and Skinner were next in line. Most likely, the murder was drug related—a hit by a rival gang. The tattoo on his neck was the only lead they had. The first forty-eight hours were crucial. Gunner had run down every lead but had no luck finding the gang connected with that tattoo. Perhaps he was wrong. Maybe the tattoo wasn't a clue. *The victim could be just a guy with a snake tattoo.*

"Why don't you go home tonight?" Skinner urged. "We'll pick this up in the morning."

"Are you sure?" Gunner asked, only to sound enthusiastic. Gunner hadn't been home in a week. Both he and Skinner had slept in beds at the precinct. He didn't like leaving his mother alone for long periods. When he was working a case or on a stakeout, she hardly ate or slept until he returned home.

"See you in the morning." Gunner grabbed his jacket from the back of his chair and cleared out of there. Sleeping in his bed never sounded so good.

The house was dark when he pulled in after midnight. He hoped that meant his mother was asleep and not pacing in the dark. After removing his shoes, he tiptoed up the stairs, trying his best not to wake her. If she woke up, there would be questions, and he was too tired to answer questions. He undressed, letting his clothes fall where they landed, and climbed into bed. The door opened, and the light from the hall flooded the room.

"I'm home. You can go back to sleep," Gunner said to the silhouette.

"You were gone for days," she answered. "I was worried."

"I have a big case," Gunner said, squinting as he looked toward the light. "Go back to bed."

"Goodnight, honey," she said before closing the door.

As tired as Gunner was, his mind drifted to Mary. A week had passed since she'd spoken harsh words, and Gunner was worried. Mary believed he'd used her. It sure looked that way. He hadn't called her. There was no plan to seduce Mary. But when he'd seen how sexy and beautiful she looked, all his common sense had gone out the window. Sex would never be casual for Mary. It was a big thing. She didn't sleep around. *I took her virginity. If she's pregnant, she'll expect a commitment. Am I ready for marriage?*

The aroma of bacon woke Gunner from sleep. When his stomach growled, he rolled over to check the time on his cell. It was ten minutes after seven. That gave him less than an hour to shower, dress, and eat. He took a quick five-minute shower, put on a suit, and hurried downstairs.

"Good morning, Mom," Gunner said before placing a kiss on her left cheek. He sat down in front of the empty plate and watched as his mother filled it with pancakes and bacon—his favorite breakfast. "You spoil me, Mom."

"Yes, I do. When are you going to meet a girl, get married, and spoil me with grandkids?"

"Maybe when I don't have to work so much," Gunner replied. *Your wishes may come sooner than you expect.* He'd eaten nothing other than takeout for the past week, and the pancakes hit the spot.

"You hinted there was a girl about a week ago," his mother continued to press.

"I was on a case. I didn't have time for a second date."

"Have you called her?"

"No. I just told you. I—"

"You haven't called her," his mother interrupted. "She's going to think—oh, forget it."

"What's she going to think?" Gunner chucked.

"If you like a girl, you call the next day."

I did more than call. A smile appeared as Gunner recalled their afternoon delight.

"It's not funny!" she yelled. "Wipe that grin off your face."

"The pancakes were great. Did you make them differently?"

"You can't change the subject, buster," his mother warned.

"I'm not." Gunner laughed. "As soon as this case is over, I'll call her."

"It may be too late already." His mother shook her head, grabbed his empty plate, then set it in the sink. "I raised you better."

Gunner stood up. "Gotta go. I don't want to be late." He kissed his mother on the cheek again before heading for the door. "I'll call if I can't make it home tonight."

Driving to work, Gunner gave what his mother said some thought. *Should I call Mary? What would I say?* Gunner released a breath. Mary had mentioned one of her mother's killers had a snake tattoo. The victim could be the man who shot her mother. He picked up the phone and dialed Skinner's number.

"I have a lead," he said when Skinner answered. "I'll let you know if it pans out." He headed to the garage to talk to Mary. The case was something he needed to do in person.

"What do you mean you haven't seen her in a week?" Gunner's voice rose. "Has anyone checked her apartment?"

"Do you know my daughter?" Joe asked.

"You're Mary's father." Gunner held out his hand, and Joe shook it. "Gunner Ryan, Detective Ryan," he corrected. "I'm working your wife's case."

"Oh, I was hoping… any new information?" Joe handed Gunner a rag to wipe off the grease he got on Gunner's hand. "Sorry."

"No problem." Gunner rubbed the grease from his hand then returned the rag. "Thanks. I just started. It's too soon to say."

"Mary and I got into an argument. I guess it upset her more than I thought, because I haven't seen her since Saturday." His tone suggested Mary's absence didn't concern him. "Mary hasn't missed a day of work in five years."

"Then why haven't you at least checked on her?" Gunner became upset.

"I figured Mary would come back once she cooled down," Joe explained. "She's stubborn like her mother."

"Can I ask what the two of you argued about?" Gunner asked.

"The Chevelle's missing. I reported it to the police on Monday. I thought maybe that's why you were here."

"No, but I hope they find it. Mary told me how much it meant to her."

"Really." Joe scowled. "She's shown no interest in it until a week ago."

For Joe's safety, Gunner didn't tell him that Mary had caught Shane trying to steal the car. *Who knows what the guy would do if backed in a corner?* Gunner planned to mention the incident to whoever the captain put in charge of the case. "Mary and I went to high school together," Gunner said, only to curb his curiosity.

"Mary only talks about JJ," Joe said. "She's very private."

"I only went one year with her. Nice to meet you." Gunner shook his hand again then hurried from the garage. If Mary hadn't missed a day of work in five years, he found it odd that her father hadn't at least called her. *What if she confronted Shane?* He hadn't seen anyone but Mary's father at the garage.

The ride to Mary's apartment only took minutes with his flasher in the window. Traffic pulled over and let him pass. He knocked on the door, waited for several seconds, then pounded again.

"Mary, are you in there?" Gunner yelled.

The door opened. Mary stood in front of him, dressed in a long pink T-shirt that met the top of her knees. "What the hell, Gunner?" Mary yawned. "Can't a girl get any sleep?"

"Why aren't you at work?" Gunner pushed his way inside. He jumped when the door closed with a slam.

"I'm on vacation," Mary answered. "What's it to you?"

"I need to talk to you." Gunner walked to the couch and sat without an invitation.

"Can we do this another time?" Mary yawned and stretched her arms. "I'm tired." Mary rolled her eyes, pushed her messy hair away from her face, and released a sigh as she plopped on the couch next to him. She crossed her arms and glared at him with an angry scowl. "So, talk." Mary wiped the sleep from her eyes and focused.

Gunner leaned forward as if he had something of significance to say. "We have a dead guy in the morgue. He has a snake tattoo."

"What does that have to do with me?" Mary shrugged.

"What? Are you kidding, Mary?" Gunner rose, and so did his voice. "You're the one that told me about the snake tattoo." When Mary didn't answer, he added, "Are you going to sit there and pretend?" He slammed his fist into his leg in frustration before lifting her from the cushion and onto her feet. "Get dressed. You're coming with me to the precinct." Gunner gave her a little nudge toward the bedroom. "This is the break you've waited ten years for."

"Fine," Mary grumbled. "But I'm taking a shower."

When Gunner opened his eyes, he found Mary studying him. "Sorry, I've been pulling doubles," Gunner said then cleared his throat. "You're right—that couch is comfortable." Gunner smiled and headed toward the door. *If only I would have slept there the first time I stayed. I wouldn't have to worry whether my actions have gotten her pregnant. Man, she's gorgeous.* "I'm stopping for doughnuts on the way. My turn to buy." When he saw Mary smiling, he added, "I don't want to hear any wisecracks about cops and doughnuts."

After a quick stop at the bakery, they headed to the precinct. Like bees to honey, detectives swarmed around the table where Gunner displayed various types of donuts. Chocolate and vanilla glazed, cinnamon rolls, crullers, apple fritters, jelly-filled, and Mary's favorite—custard-filled.

Gunner held them at bay. "The lady goes first."

"Custard," Mary replied.

Gunner took a small paper plate from the stack. Using a napkin, he pulled the custard-filled long john from the box and placed it on top. A second after he handed the plate to Mary, the men begin grabbing their selections. Mary wondered how long it had been since they'd eaten, because when they walked away, only two doughnuts remained.

"I guess I'm having a glazed." Gunner sighed when all that remained was glazed and jelly-filled. "I was craving a cinnamon roll."

"I'll trade you if you like custard?" Mary offered.

"No, thank you. Could I get you a cup of coffee?"

"I thought I came here to see the tattoo?"

"Patience," Gunner advised.

"Fine. I would like tea," Mary said.

Gunner left and returned a few minutes later with two Styrofoam cups with tea bag strings hanging over the edges. "Since I forgot to ask, I brought cream and sugar," Gunner announced as he pulled packets of sugar and containers of half-and-half.

"Where's your partner?" Mary asked. She scanned the room and saw a dozen or so detectives stuffing their mouths but no Skinner.

"Good question," Gunner said. He went to the box that contained the last jelly donut and closed it. "Better save him one." He set it on the desk opposite his before returning to his seat. "Are you upset with me for some reason?"

After taking a bite of her long john, Mary eyed him with suspicion. "No," she lied. Mary removed the tea bag from the cup and set it on the napkin next to the custard roll. She ripped open two sugar packets, poured them in, then dumped in one whole container of cream.

Gunner did the same and smiled. "I like loads of cream in my tea too." He stirred his then handed the spoon to Mary. "If the guy in the morgue is your mother's killer, it will be a big lead." He blew on his tea before taking a sip.

"If there's a guy in the morgue?" Mary's eyes narrowed again. "If you're worried about what happens between us—"

"No," Gunner interrupted. "Let's not discuss that here." He scanned the room for eavesdroppers. He had an image to uphold. How would it look to his coworkers and especially the captain if he had gotten an innocent woman like Mary pregnant? They already called him a pretty boy. In school, he was king. At the precinct, he was the low man on the totem pole. The phone on his desk vibrated. It was the morgue, telling him it was okay to bring Mary. The victim was pretty bloody, and Gunner didn't want to shock Mary. Just seeing a dead body was hard for anyone to stomach. Hell, Gunner vomited when viewing his first corpse. A woman had been murdered—stabbed multiple times in the chest. It was a gruesome scene. "The medical examiner is ready for us. Finish your tea," Gunner urged when he saw Mary had finished the doughnut. Gunner shoved the last of his vanilla-glazed doughnut in his mouth and took a swallow of tea. He watched Mary force down her tea.

"I'm not a fast drinker," she whined. "How come you don't have to drink your tea?" Mary asked, sounding like a kid.

"Leave it. Let's go." Gunner led Mary through the department without saying a word until they reached the elevators. "After you."

He wanted to take Mary into his arms and kiss her the second the doors closed, but he refrained. He was unsure if Mary would approve. Her attitude toward him led him to believe she wouldn't even go on a date if he asked. "Prepare yourself. It can be unsettling to see a dead body," Gunner said when the doors opened.

They followed the posted signs to the morgue. The hall seemed to get colder as they walked nearer. At the end of the hall, they met up with a man in a white coat. His name tag identified him as Dr. Hanson, the medical examiner. The doctor led them into a well-lit white room. One wall was covered in stainless steel and had at least a dozen little doors with latches. Dr. Hanson opened one in the middle. With one pull, a body covered in a white sheet slid out.

"Would you rather I show you some pictures?" Gunner asked when Mary trembled.

"No, I'm just cold."

When the medical examiner lifted the sheet, Mary's eyes rounded. After several seconds of showing no emotion, she ran from the room.

"Thanks, Hanson!" Gunner yelled as he left to follow Mary. He caught up with her at the elevator. "I'm sorry. Seeing a dead body can be… are you okay, Mary?" The elevator opened, and Mary hurried in. Gunner followed, never taking his eyes off her. "Did you recognize him?"

When Mary broke down into tears, he wrapped his arms around her. "I'm sorry," Gunner repeated as Mary shook in his arms. "Talk to me."

The elevators opened, and Gunner backed away when he saw the stares. The detectives already called him a pretty boy and teased him about the attention he got from women. What would they think after witnessing his arms around a woman?

Mary ran out of the elevator and through the squad room. Gunner followed at a slower pace. He worried it might look like a lover's spat or as if she'd turned down his unsolicited advances. Mary was leaning against his car when he caught up. When Gunner tried to touch her, she pushed him away.

"Please, just take me home. I don't want to talk about it," Mary snapped.

When he unlocked the car, Mary climbed in.

"But, Mary, is he the man or not?" Gunner asked as soon as he was sitting beside her.

"No, now take me home."

The ride back to her apartment seemed to take forever. The cop in Gunner wanted to push her further, get some answers, but he worried that seeing a dead body had traumatized her. Even though he needed to know what direction to take his case, he decided to give Mary a day or so before pressing. "I'll call you in a few days," Gunner announced as Mary stepped from the car.

"Whatever." Mary shrugged and closed the door.

Chapter Five

Two days had passed, and Mary had finished an entire bag of M&M's while waiting for a call from Gunner. She felt relieved and disappointed at the same time—thankful she didn't have to explain why seeing the dead man upset her and disappointed that after their afternoon of making love, Gunner didn't miss her. The tattoo on the dead man's neck was the same as the one on Shane's and the one on the man who'd killed her mother. The information would most likely help Gunner and bring him closer to solving her mother's murder. A part of her didn't want him to solve it. Hatred for the man who'd shot her mother had pushed her to achieve a black belt in martial arts. Karate had taught her discipline—a way to keep her fear and anger at bay. But finding out Shane had been involved the whole time made her blood boil. Mary wanted to go back to work and beat the truth out of him.

A phone call from the auto body shop brought her out of her head. Mary avoided answering the calls from her father. She planned to return to work soon, or he would have to replace her.

"Hey, Mary," Carl Web said in a happy tone.

"Hey, Carl. Is there a problem?"

"No, just wanted to tell you we got farther than expected. We are ready to paint."

"Already? Wow." Mary was surprised. "It's only been a week."

"Well, other than replacing the windows, the car didn't need much bodywork."

"And the interior?" Mary dreaded having to ask. Her mother's blood had stained the seats and dried on the leather and carpet. The shop had to clean or replace the fabric, but it felt like they were washing away her mother's memory.

"We replaced the carpet and sent the seat out to have it recovered. The upholstery we can pick up by the end of the week," Carl explained. "We just have to know the color."

Mary sighed. Black was the color her mother had wanted it. But for her plan to work, she would have to paint it. Her father and Shane had to believe someone had stolen it. If the car remained black, the bad guys would suspect her—the little girl they wanted to hunt down and kill.

"Mary?" Carl said. "Are you still there?"

"Oh, sorry, can I have another day to think about it?"

"We can wait as long as you want, but if you want it done by the weekend, I need to know tomorrow morning."

"I'll call you before ten," Mary said.

The phone rang in her hand before she had the time to set it down. It was her father. She had to talk to him sooner or later. She took in a breath and answered, "Hello."

"Finally. Where in the hell have you been?" Joe asked. "Agnes and I were starting to worry."

"I've lived in the same apartment for the past four years," Mary flung at him. The phone became quiet. Mary thought he'd hung up until she heard him release a loud sigh.

"Are you coming back to work soon?"

"Tomorrow," Mary answered. "Sorry. I haven't been feeling well."

"Oh, I thought… I'm sorry about your mother's car," he said in a much softer tone.

"Yeah, me too. I'm sure the police will find it."

"Yeah, you're probably right."

"I'll be there at nine," Mary said before hanging up. She wasn't ready to face her father or Shane, but she needed to keep an eye on Shane to make them believe everything was back to normal. The day sped by, and if she hadn't gone outside to get some fresh air, Mary wouldn't have noticed. Mary walked out onto the balcony in time to witness the pink sky turn the clouds to lavender before the sun disappeared beneath them. The sunset explained the rumbling in her tummy. Pizza would hit the spot, and it would be nice to get out. A warm summer's night drive and pizza in the park could help her decide the color to paint the Chevelle. *Red with black stripes. Silver with black stripes. Maybe blue without stripes on the hood.* Her brain felt like it might explode. The Chevelle's black interior left Mary with endless possibilities. She ordered a large pizza with three meat toppings. Protein was what she needed to help her brain choose.

Forty-five minutes later, Mary was in her car, eating pizza in the dark, parked under a large maple tree on the edge of the empty parking lot and hidden from the overhead light. When lights appeared, her eyes followed the vehicle as it drove to the opposite end of the lot and shut off its lights. The dark car resembled a Cadillac, but Mary couldn't tell for sure. She didn't want to alert them to her presence, but a voice in her head told her to leave. Mary closed the lid on the pizza box and placed her hand on the ignition. A second car pulled in and parked next to the black car with gold stripes—it looked very similar to a Chevelle. She was trying to recall where she'd seen the vehicle before when music blasted from her phone. It was a love song she'd placed on the phone to tell her it was Gunner calling. The tune reminded Mary of his lovemaking. Her heart skipped a beat because it startled her—and because it was Gunner. She hoped whoever was in those cars didn't see the light or hear it. *Why would he call at ten thirty at night? Did he want to come over for a quick roll in the hay?*

"Stop it, Mary." She rejected the call, turned it to vibrate, and turned her attention to the vehicles. Two men got out, and both opened their trunks. They unloaded something from the striped car into the back of the sedan. Mary suspected drugs.

Her cell vibrated. Gunner was calling again. She rejected the call, then a few seconds later, a text came in. Gunner said he was at her apartment and wanted her to answer the door. Mary sent a text saying she wasn't at home. The two men returned to their cars. Seconds later, the dark sedan raced out of the lot. The striped car followed but passed under the light. Mary got a closer look at the car but not the man inside. Her phone vibrated again.

"What do you want, Gunner?" she yelled.

"I wanted to make sure you are all right," he said.

"Why would you even care?" Mary answered with an attitude.

"Your father says you haven't returned to work all week."

"You called my father?" Mary yelled. *What if my father finds out about the tattoo? What if my father knows about Shane's tattoo or sees it? It could put his life in danger.* Mary concluded she had no choice but to tell Gunner. "I'm not home. Can we meet at my apartment?"

"I haven't left yet. I thought you were lying to avoid me."

"See you in fifteen," Mary said before hanging up. To be on the safe side, she waited a few more minutes before pulling out. Seeing the black-and-gold car that looked like the Chevelle had been like having a déjà vu moment. Where she'd last seen the vehicle came to her in a flash. The car was a '69 Skylark, and it had been in the garage a day before her mother's murder. *Is that how Shane is selling drugs? Did he put the drugs in the Skylark the day before my mother's murder, and they mixed up the cars?* The man's words rang in her head. "Open the trunk. Give us the drugs."

A horn brought Mary out of the flashback. Mary swerved to miss the car and pulled her car back to the right side of the road. The near miss caused her heart to beat double time. She took in a few deep breaths to calm her heart, slow her pulse, and focus on the road.

At the apartment complex, Gunner had parked in one of two spots assigned to her apartment. She pulled into the second, turned off the engine, and took in a breath. *Are you ready to talk to Gunner? Are you going to tell him everything or only enough to keep Dad safe?* A tap on her window caused her to jump. Gunner stood outside, looking down at her. *God, I would have given anything in high school to have him show up at my house.*

She lifted the pizza box and her purse off the seat and opened the door. "Went out for pizza," Mary said. His presence made her heart skip a beat. He had to be one of the most handsome men she'd ever met. His lovemaking left her wanting more.

"Let me help," Gunner said, taking the pizza box out of her hand. "Anthony's make the best pizza."

"All meat. Have some," Mary said.

"Thanks, but I'll wait until we're inside." Gunner followed closely and refrained from talking until they were inside the apartment. "I figured I would give you a few days to calm down before talking to you," he said as he set the box on the table.

Mary went straight to the cupboard and pulled out a plate. "I didn't realize I was upset." Mary dropped the dish on the table, proving her statement to be false. "Would you like something to drink?"

"Whatever's easiest." Gunner smiled at her.

"I have wine," Mary announced. She walked to the refrigerator and pulled a bottle of Moscato from the shelf. "Oh, I have a cola too."

"A cola is fine," Gunner said as he walked to the balcony. He gave the sliding door a shove. "You shouldn't leave that open. Burglars would have no trouble climbing."

"On the second floor?" Mary sounded surprised.

"You'd be surprised at how agile they are. I investigated a burglary where a man climbed three stories. Of course, there was a tree next to the window."

Mary handed him the bottle. "Help yourself. Or do you want me to reheat it?"

"No, I like it cold," Gunner replied.

Mary grabbed a glass from the cupboard while Gunner placed two slices on the plate and sat in the chair. "Most girls like veggies on their pizza." He took a bite and smiled. "This is good."

Mary popped the cork and filled the wine glass to the top. "Eat all you like. Just save me two slices for lunch tomorrow." Her eyes closed as she drank the bubbly. The Moscato was supposed to be for JJ's birthday, but Mary needed it tonight to calm her nerves. "Would you like some?"

"Yes, but can't. I'm on the job," Gunner said when Mary gave him a sideways glance and a doubtful look. "I'm on my dinner break." They sat in silence until Gunner finished his third slice. "Wow, I'm stuffed." He patted his belly, picked up the plate, and carried it to the sink. "Can we talk?" he asked after setting the plate in the sink. His eyes rounded when he saw Mary empty her third glass. Gunner placed his hand over the top when Mary tried to pour another. "We can't discuss the case if you're drunk."

"I'm not drunk." Mary blinked as she looked him in the eye. She felt a little tipsy as she placed the bottle in the refrigerator. After taking a breath to calm her emotions, she followed, giving him her full attention when joining him on the couch. "Yes, the tattoo's the same."

"But you told me it wasn't." Gunner's voice elevated.

"I lied. Seeing the dead man and the tattoo frightened me." Mary matched his tone and stood.

Gunner reached for her hand and stood to comfort her. Mary sank into him. Not because she loved the woodsy smell of his cologne or how soothing it felt to be in his arms—it was because she could barely stand. She'd planned to share it with JJ because she could never finish it independently—she rarely drank.

Gunner's mouth covered hers, filling her body with excitement. He pulled away suddenly. "I can't, Mary," he whispered. "I'm due back at work in less than an hour."

Did he think I was seducing him? He was the one who kissed me. One more second in his arms, and she would've asked Gunner to take her to bed. Why did he affect her this way? Gunner was a chocolate addiction—like M&M's, Mary could never stop at only one. Her craving ached to be satisfied. Mary's temper flared. She left his side and stood by the door. "You'd better go."

"Maybe we should talk at the precinct tomorrow. That way, we won't end up in bed," Gunner said in a humorous tone before opening the door. "See you tomorrow, then?" He stood in the doorway, waiting for her answer.

"I can't," Mary replied.

"We need to discuss this." Gunner stepped toward her, becoming more persistent.

"I have to return to work in the morning. I don't want to lose my job."

Gunner chuckled. "Your father wouldn't fire you."

When Mary's eyes met his, she told him the truth, hoping he would let her off. "I've missed a week and a half already."

"I work afternoons. You could come after work," Gunner said.

"Fine, see you around six." Mary gave him attitude.

***

All three lines were ringing when Mary opened at nine. "Kelly Auto. Can you hold please?" Mary asked each line without giving them a chance to respond. Mary reached for the appointment book on the shelf below the phone, but it was missing. As the three lines blinked, she searched every ledge and found nothing.

"What the hell?" Mary grabbed the scrap paper she used to jot things down throughout the day, and that box, too, was missing. Her temper boiled. "I leave for a week, and everything falls apart," she grumbled. She dashed from the showroom into the garage to find something to write on. Her father hadn't unlocked the office. His head was under a hood, repairing a carburetor, and Shane was underneath a truck in the second bay. Mary ran back to the front for her set of keys, and two more customers had come in, and the phones were still blinking. She pulled a small pad of sticky notes from her purse. "I'll be right with you," Mary said to the people waiting. "Sorry for the wait," she said to each person in the line. The third line hung up before Mary could get to them. She jotted down each appointment on a sticky note, having no clue if the time was available, and waited on the people in front of her. The first customer needed a set of tires. The second a new muffler.

An hour and ten customers later, Mary had filled the window behind her with bright-orange sticky notes. Two customers waited to be next in line to have their vehicles serviced. Without the appointment book, Mary had no clue if the garage could work them in. She grabbed the keys from her purse and left the counter to find the appointment book, hoping that her father made appointments from his office in her absence. Mary felt around the cluttered desk for an appointment book. When she didn't find one, she searched through each drawer. Seeing both the appointment book and a stack of new invoices in the top left-hand drawer, she grabbed them and hurried back to the showroom.

It took her about thirty minutes to enter the sticky notes and reschedule a few appointments. After listening to her stomach growl for hours, Mary got the chance to eat her lunch around three. Chicken salad never tasted so good. While nibbling on the carrots, she straightened the invoices that her father left scattered across his desk.

The morning chaos made Mary realize how wrong it was to have left her father hanging for the past week. It was hard enough for him to fix the cars, let alone mind the front and schedule appointments. It was after four when she returned the invoices to her father's desk. When placing them in the basket designated for completed work, she sat in his seat, recalling all the times she straightened the invoices as a child.

It had been years since he tricked her into helping. The day before her mother's murder came to mind. After her father showed Mary the gift he bought for her mother, he tricked her into cleaning off his desk to help to pay for it. What happened to the present?

Mary opened the top drawer where he kept it that day. It was gone. She continued to search and stopped at the bottom drawer. Someone wrapped the small cardboard box in shiny purple paper with a white bow. The last time Mary laid eyes on it, greasy fingerprints covered the box. Mary hid it under her blouse, returned to the front, then stuck the present inside her purse. When she looked up, her father was standing in front of the counter.

"It's nice to have you back," he said. "I missed you."

"Sorry, Dad. When I heard about the Chevelle... well, I guess it bothered me more than I thought."

"I understand. The car was something your mother wanted you to have." Her father walked around the counter. "I miss her too," he whispered before pulling Mary into his arms.

"Miss who?" Agnes asked.

Her presence startled them both. Her father backed away as if Mary had suddenly poked him with electricity. "No one," Joe lied. "What are you doing here so early?"

"It's almost five. You promised to come straight home early and take Josh to soccer practice."

"It's that time already?" Joe looked at the clock on the wall. It read 4:56.

"Don't worry, Dad. I'll lock up."

"Thanks, honey," Joe said before placing a kiss on her forehead. "Thanks again for coming in. The days are easier when you're here." He hurried out the door and into Agnes's car. The fluorescent lime-green shirt Josh was wearing glowed from the back seat.

Mary waved to Josh as they drove past the window. When she turned to lock up, Shane stood before her.

"Nice to see you back, Mary." Shane smiled then asked where she'd been all week.

"Home. Why?" She stared into his eyes.

"You didn't go on vacation somewhere?"

"No. Why?" Mary wasn't giving him any information on her personal life. "Can't I take a week off? I've never taken a vacation."

"Me either," Shane replied, sounding defensive.

"Why is that, Shane? Why haven't you ever taken a vacation?" Mary looked him in the eye, giving him attitude. Then she turned away to hide her emotions. Mary wanted to accuse him of selling drugs and killing her mother, but she held her tongue. She reached into her purse for the keys to the front entrance and walked to it. "Well?" Mary asked while turning the key.

"I can't afford it." Shane shrugged. "Your dad can't afford to pay for a week's vacation."

"I'm sure he would give it to you if you asked." Mary walked straight to the cash register, turned the key to the letter Z, and pushed the total button. The drawer slid out, and Mary set it on the counter while waiting for the totals to print. She reached for an empty bag to put her deposit in and sat it on top of the drawer. The tape told Mary how much money she'd taken in and the totals of each category. Repairs had taken in the most, followed by tire sales. "I need to lock up before I count the bag."

"Would you like me to wait?" Shane asked.

"Why would I do that?" Mary asked. "Never needed anyone to watch over me before."

"Well, with the Chevelle missing, I was worried about another break-in."

"I'm sure the police will find it. How hard could it be to find a car like that?" Mary kept a cool head. She picked up the cash drawer and carried it to her father's office. She usually would count it out front, but she wanted to get rid of him.

He followed her to the office and stood in the doorway. "Yeah, you're probably right. From what I hear from your dad, it was quite the car."

Mary continued to count, starting with the coins to put in the drawer for the next day. They would start with one hundred fifty even in the drawer each day, so Mary had to subtract from what she put in the bag that would go to the bookkeeper. Mary stopped counting and answered his question before continuing. "Yes, I was looking forward to learning how to drive it."

"You don't know how to drive it?" Shane gave her a suspicious glance.

"I was only twelve when she died," Mary pointed out. "I never got the chance to learn how to drive a stick shift. She was going to teach me."

"So, it was a manual transmission?"

"Yes, why?"

"Because that limits who can steal it. There are a lot of people that don't know how to drive a stick." Shane smiled.

"Is it that hard?" Mary asked. She had to learn something next week if she wanted to drive it from the body shop to the storage garage where she planned to hide it.

"Not for me but to someone inexperienced," Shane said, almost bragging.

"Well, maybe you could teach me. That's if the police find it." Mary had to recount the pennies. She stopped and looked up at Shane. "If you don't mind, I need to count this."

"Oh, have a hot date or something?" Shane teased.

"I have somewhere to be." It wasn't as if Mary could tell Shane she was going to the police station to talk to them about the crime he'd committed.

"I was hoping I could take you to dinner," Shane said.

"What?" Mary's eyes rounded. His invitation had taken her by surprise. "Why would you want to do that?"

"I've wanted to ask ever since you turned eighteen. I finally got the courage."

Mary eyed him sideways. Shane had always been friendly to her. Until learning of his deceit, Mary had thought of him as a big brother. It wasn't as if he was unattractive. Mary only saw him in greasy overalls, dirty hands, and an oily baseball cap. Last week at Josh's party was the first time she'd seen him cleaned up. Shane removed his hat and tucked it under his arm. He ran his hand through his dark waves, and they bounced in place. His brown eyes were dark and mysterious.

"Aren't you a little old for me?" Mary asked, hoping he would agree.

"Only six years," Shane answered. "That's not much."

Mary put her hands under the desk to hide the shaking. "Shane, I don't think my father would approve." Using most of her nerve, she met his round eyes. "What if it didn't work out? One of us would have to quit, and it wouldn't be me."

He left his spot by the door and walked toward her. "You're probably right." He shrugged. "Sorry, I just thought since we had a lot in common... well, never mind." His face reddened.

"Shane, you're like a big brother to me."

"I was hoping for more. Can I at least get a hug?"

Mary wanted to kick his ass and tell him that if he touched her, she would kill him. Instead, she stood and let Shane wrap his arms around her. The smell of motor oil and breath mints filled her nostrils. His touch and his smell sickened her. Her body stiffened. "We can still be friends, right?" She faked a smile. "I've just started dating someone recently."

"You don't have to lie, Mary," Shane said before taking a step backward. "I'm a man. Not a boy. I can take rejection."

"He's not a boy," Mary said, thinking of Gunner. "That's why I was hurrying. I have a date tonight. He expects me at six. I'm late."

"Why didn't you bring him to Josh's birthday party?"

"He had to work." Mary thought telling a half-truth was better than a complete lie. "As I said, we've just started dating." All Mary wanted to do was go home and take a shower after Shane touched her. "Sorry, Shane, I have to finish. I'll lock up."

"Can't blame a guy for trying." He shrugged.

"Sorry, you're a nice guy. My father and I appreciate all the help you've given us over the years—especially after my mom's death," Mary said. Her lips twitched as she fought to hold her smile.

"See you tomorrow," Shane said with a nod. Then he left the garage like his pants were on fire.

Mary waited until Shane drove out of the parking lot before locking the back door. *What the hell was that?* It seemed suspicious. Why would Shane make a play for her now? Did he suspect she knew the truth? Did Shane want to take her to dinner to find out what she knew? No, Shane wasn't aware she knew he was involved with the men who'd murdered her mother. Were his feelings for her the reason he hadn't let his buddy kill her? Or was it because someone had stolen the Chevelle, and he didn't want the cops snooping around?

Mary returned to the office to count her cashbox. She placed the counted drawer inside the safe and dropped the money bag into a separate slot for the bookkeeper.

It was six thirty when she climbed behind the wheel. Would Gunner think she wasn't coming? She'd planned to stop at the sandwich shop near the precinct. Since they closed at six, she pulled into a burger joint, ordered two burgers and two iced teas in case Gunner hadn't had the chance to eat dinner.

Gunner's face showed surprise when Mary arrived. "Mary," he exclaimed as she entered the station. "Have a seat." He pulled out the chair in front of the desk. "Do I smell food?"

"I stopped for a burger." She set the drink carrier and the bag containing the burgers on top of his desk and sat. "Have you eaten?"

"No, I usually take a lunch break at eight." He sat in his chair and pushed it closer to the desk. "But I can take it early. I didn't have time for lunch."

"It's only a burger and iced tea." Mary shrugged.

"My belly's rumbling," Gunner said while patting it.

Mary opened her burger, took a bite, then laid it on the paper wrapper. She watched Gunner do the same. "My burger tastes good," Mary said when he stared at her. "Sorry I'm late. My dad left early to take Josh to a soccer game. I stayed to close up."

"I was about to call you when I saw you walk in," Gunner told her.

They ate in silence. Mary focused on the other detectives so she wouldn't have to look at Gunner. "Hello," Mary said when Detective Skinner came to tell Gunner he was taking his dinner break. Skinner said hello in return and left without any further conversation. "I don't think he likes me much."

"Skinner?" Gunner chuckled. "He doesn't like most everyone."

"I thought being nice was part of the job," Mary replied.

"If you want people to cough up information, you do," Gunner admitted. "Oh, Mary, that isn't why I'm nice to you."

"Why are you?" Mary's eyes narrowed with distrust. Was taking her to bed a way to get her to talk? If the guy in the morgue had showed up before he'd agreed to work on her mother's murder, it would have put Gunner's motives into question. Hell, she'd questioned his motives before that. Mary didn't understand why a handsome, sexy guy like Gunner even gave her the time of day. His confession that he'd found her attractive in high school had left her stunned.

"I thought I made that clear the other night," Gunner hinted.

Does he mean his story about seeing me outside the gymnasium in a pink dress or the night he took my virginity? Stop it, Mary. Don't rush to judge. "So why am I here tonight?" Mary asked after clearing her throat and her mind.

"The tattoo," Gunner said. He sat the iced tea on the desk. "You were going to explain why you lied to me."

"I never lied to you!" Mary yelled.

The room became silent. Several detectives stopped what they were doing to look at her. Gunner held up his hand as if telling them everything was okay, and everyone went on with business as usual.

"I never lied," Mary said in a lower tone. "I just didn't tell you everything. There's a difference."

Gunner shook his head. "I never thought a practicing Catholic girl would lie. Isn't it a sin or something?" He laughed.

"Well, I never thought I would sleep with the first guy that stuck his tongue in my mouth either," Mary slung at him snidely.

"Keep your voice down," Gunner whispered. He scanned the room before continuing. When no one paid them any mind, Gunner asked, "I was your first kiss too?"

"Are you bragging, or do you just want me to feel like a slut?"

"I thought meeting here would keep it casual between us," Gunner said.

Mary released a breath. "Sorry, after the Shane thing... I guess I'm angry with the wrong man."

"The Shane thing?" Gunner's eyebrows met in the center.

"Oh, nothing." Mary sighed again. "He asked me out tonight," Mary told him only to make him jealous. There was no comparison between the two. Gunner would win out every time. "Can we finish this? I'm tired."

"What did you say?"

"I said yes." Mary rolled her eyes then snapped, "What the hell do you think I said?"

Gunner eyed her sideways, rolled his chair backward, and opened a drawer in his desk. "Take a look at this," he said before dropping a photo of the tattoo on the dead man's neck. "Is it the same or not?"

Mary lifted the photograph and brought it closer to study it. "Yes, Shane has one on his chest just like it." Mary set it in front of Gunner.

"So Shane is connected." Gunner rubbed the stubble on his chin and remained quiet for at least a minute. "Could they be running drugs or something out of the garage?"

"Drugs," Mary said.

"Why? Have you seen evidence of this?" Gunner gave her his full attention.

"No, I rarely go into the garage area." When Gunner gave her a doubting look, she added, "I work mostly in the front showroom selling tires, answering the phone, and scheduling appointments. You know—girl stuff."

"Girl stuff." Gunner chuckled. "What do you mean?"

"Oh, nothing," Mary shrugged and released a breath. "My father won't allow me to fix anything. He thinks a woman shouldn't get their nails dirty." Mary leaned back and crossed her arms.

"Why would you want to get those pretty hands of yours dirty?" Gunner mocked.

"You too?" Mary asked.

Gunner leaned in and whispered, "I just meant your hands and your body were soft when we made love."

Mary's face flushed. She gazed into Gunner's eyes. They were round, mysterious, and the color of a turquoise sea. Mary's body trembled. If they weren't in the middle of a station of cops, she would lean in for a kiss—not just a quick, simple peck but one that involved tongues, arms, and maybe sex on top of the desk. "Your eyes are blue today," she whispered.

Gunner cleared his throat and leaned backward. "They change color when I wear certain shades of blue sometimes."

His eyes were gorgeous. Mary wanted to tell him so but needed to calm what was happening between them. She straightened, forgetting why she was upset in the first place. "Is identifying the tattoo all you wanted from me?"

"Yes, but can you tell me why you were so upset a minute ago?" Gunner probed.

"It's not important."

"If it concerns you, it's important to me."

Gunner's mouth turned up at the edges. Mary couldn't tell if he was serious or only trying to charm her. The attraction she had for him clouded her ability to read him. "I'm just as smart as any guy—maybe most guys—when it comes to fixing a car, but my father gives me no credit."

"Do you want a raise or something?" Gunner replied.

"No—yes—that's not the point I'm trying to make." Mary sighed and brought her hands to her head before balling them into fists at her sides. "Take the other day, for example. A man came in for new tires. I checked the treads, listened to the engine, and asked him questions. I told him he needed new tires and possibly a wheel alignment by the way they were worn. He told me the car was pulling, especially when braking, so I told him he might need new tie rods or ball joints. He laughed and said he needed to talk to a man."

"That chauvinist," Gunner teased.

"It's not funny. It happens to me all the time." Mary stood. "I was right. Also, when I listened to his engine, I could tell his timing was off slightly."

"Sit down, Mary." Gunner stood, still seeming to find Mary's declaration humorous. "Most men don't like it if a woman is better at something. Someday, it will change."

After Mary took her seat, Gunner checked for eavesdroppers. "I bet by if anyone saw these hands, they would say I couldn't sew. I can't, but I knit a pretty mean scarf."

"Gunner Ryan, a knitter." Mary giggled. "I won't tell," Mary whispered. They both laughed.

"My mother taught me," he admitted, almost bragging. "I can also knit nice hot pads."

"The next time I bake a batch of cookies, I'll think of you," Mary teased.

"You bake?" Gunner asked, suggesting he would like to see for himself.

"I make the best oatmeal chocolate chip this side of Michigan," Mary bragged. "My mother's recipe."

"See what mothers can teach us?" Gunner said without thinking, "Sorry," he added when Mary became distant.

"That's okay."

They were silent for a moment.

"Why did I come here again? Oh, the tattoos." Mary checked the time on her phone. She and Gunner had talked for over an hour. "I'll snoop around the garage and see if I can figure out what Shane has been up to," Mary said as she left her seat. "Maybe take him up on that date."

"No—I mean, you could put yourself in danger," Gunner said.

"What's he going to do?" Mary snickered. "Have you forgotten I can protect myself?" Mary turned on her heel and headed for the door.

Gunner followed. He hurried in front of her and opened the door. "Don't do anything foolish," he said and continued to walk beside her. "I'll continue to investigate the man in the morgue. Maybe his murder will lead us to solve two murders."

"You didn't have to walk me to my car," Mary said when they stopped next to the door.

"It's dark." Gunner pulled Mary into his arms with one quick movement and planted a lengthy kiss on her mouth. "I'll call you." He released her and added "Good night" in a sexy voice before leaving her standing beside the car. Gunner's sexy voice sent a tingle to her heart. With the warmth of his lips lingering on hers, Mary climbed behind the wheel. As she drove back to the apartment, she wondered if Gunner would still want her after she killed the people responsible for her mother's death. Deep in her heart, she questioned whether God would understand.

Chapter Six

The ringing phone woke Mary early the next morning. It was a good thing because she had forgotten to set her alarm the night before. The body shop needed her to choose a color to paint the Chevelle. Red with black strips, she decided, would be appropriate for revenge. Revenge was what Mary had wanted her entire life, and when the body shop had completed the work on the Chevelle, vengeance was what she would seek.

The garage was busy when she arrived. People often dropped off their cars the night before or before they opened, so her father and Shane could get started at eight. The showroom didn't open till nine. Mary performed her regular procedures, like counting the cash drawer and the safe, before opening. With twenty minutes to spare, she delayed turning on the overhead lights and strolled out to the garage to talk to her father or see if he needed help.

"Hi, sweetie." Her father lifted his head from underneath the hood of the 1957 Chevy Bel Air.

"What a beauty." Mary walked around the red-and-white car, admiring the color and bodywork. "Kudos to whoever did the restoration. The paint job is flawless." Mary walked to the driver's-side window and looked inside. The roomy interior matched the outside—red and white. "Can I sit in it?"

"Go ahead," her father encouraged. He wiped his hands and followed. "This one had a full restoration. It must have cost them a pretty penny."

"Oh, but it was worth it," Mary said as she ran her hand over the newly recovered bench seat. "They sure knew how to build them back then." Mary's eyes followed the dash, admiring the chrome that went from one side to the other. She reached for the knob on the radio and turned it on. "It works."

"Why wouldn't it?" her father asked. "I told you the owner did a full restoration."

"I like that the glove box is in the middle. I have trouble reaching mine sometimes." Mary turned the latch in the compartment and found an updated stereo system capable of playing CDs and a place to plug in an auxiliary cable. "Nice." When her dad left the window, Mary's eyes met Shane's. "Hello, Shane," she called, faking a smile.

When he didn't answer, Mary climbed out of the car and strolled over to the car's front in the next bay. Shane glanced her way but continued to work on the carburetor. "Does it need a new one?"

"The throttle was sticking. I gave it a few sprays of cleaner, and it seems to be working fine now."

"Need any help?"

Shane stopped and eyed her sideways. "The princess shouldn't get her nails dirty."

"Oh, that's how you want to play it?" Mary sneered. "The timing is off a couple of clicks." Mary's lip curled as she walked away. "Got to open," she announced when passing her father. She jumped when her father closed the solid hood of the '57.

Sales and scheduling appointments kept Mary busy throughout the morning. When business slowed, she skipped out to the sandwich shop up the road and returned with turkey subs for everyone. She ate lunch out front while her father and Shane sat in his office. A few minutes before closing, her father announced Josh had a soccer game and left Mary alone with Shane. After locking and cashing out her till, she ran into Shane, who was peeling off his coveralls. "Do you have plans tonight?"

"Nope." Shane's reply was short.

"Want to go to the diner up the road and get a burger?" Mary asked. She stood in the doorway of her father's office and watched him hang the coveralls on a hook. "They make great burgers there."

When he didn't answer, she went inside and began counting. Fifteen minutes later, she came back, and Shane had gone. Mary locked the office door, grabbed her purse from the shelf under the cash register, and headed out the back entrance. After switching off the lights and setting the alarm, she locked the door and headed out to her car. To her surprise, Shane was sitting on the tailgate of his truck. "Did you change your mind?"

"After I thought about your invitation for a while, a burger sounded good." Shane pulled his keys from his pocket. "We can take my truck," Shane insisted.

"I can take mine and meet you there," Mary said. If she took her own car, she wouldn't be in a situation where she couldn't leave if she wanted. Being alone with Shane was something she tried to avoid.

"Why take two vehicles?" He tossed the keys in the air and caught them. "Come on, hop in."

Mary wanted to take separate cars, but she didn't push the issue. "This is nice," Mary said, making small talk. "How long have you owned this truck?"

"About three years. I bought it new," Shane bragged. "You've seen it parked in the lot every day."

"Yes, but I never saw the interior. Pretty fancy." Mary was referring to the heated leather seats, automatic windows, and computer in the dashboard. "I pictured you driving with the bare minimum. No carpet, rubber mats on the floors, and crank windows."

"Really?" Shane chuckled. "How little you know about me."

They drove to the diner in silence. Mary faced out the window, thinking she'd made a mistake. Yes, she could probably kick his ass if he tried anything but not if he had a gun. She wanted to check the glove compartment for a weapon, but what excuse could she use to open it?

"Hello, Mary," the waitress said. "Booth or table?"

"Booth," Mary and Shane said at the same time.

They passed a glass case displaying several kinds of pies. Mary's mouth watered when she saw the cheesecake topped with cherries. The waitress seated them in a booth next to the window and took their beverage order before leaving. Mary stared out the window, trying to find a way to work his tattoo into the conversation. "Have you ever eaten here before?"

"Once, a long time ago. The waitress knew you by name." Shane smiled.

Mary had no clue how the waitress knew her name. She's only eaten at the diner twice. A few months back, she'd come in alone and sat on a stool at the counter. The second time had been with Gunner. "Only a couple of times." Mary smiled at him, letting Shane believe what he wanted. Then Mary remembered selling her a set of tires a few months back. They'd talked to fill the time while she waited for them to be mounted.

She and Shane ordered a burgers and fries when the waitress returned and went back to awkwardly staring at each other. "So, what are your hobbies? What do you do when you leave work?"

"Not much," Shane replied.

"You're making it hard for me," Mary teased. "I hang out with my friend JJ." She didn't want to tell him anything too personal. "We go to the theater sometimes."

"Don't care for movies much." Shane shrugged. "I'm usually too tired when I leave work to do anything."

"Sorry, do we work you too hard?" Mary asked, faking caring.

The door opened—a bell attached to the door alerted everyone. Mary's jaw dropped when Gunner strolled in with another woman. She pretended not to notice him. The waitress arrived with their meals, blocking her view of Gunner.

"How are your tires holding up, Jessica?" Mary asked only to keep Gunner from seeing her.

"You remembered my name." She smiled. "They're holding up nicely. Thanks for asking." She sat their meals on the table in front of them then asked if they needed anything else. Shane held up the empty ketchup bottle and asked for more. The waitress grabbed a full one off the open tables next to them then asked if they wanted anything else.

"No, we're good," Mary said in a friendly tone. "Thanks." When Jessica stepped away, her eyes met Gunner's. He nodded an acknowledgment then gave his full attention to his date.

"No. Your father gave me a job when I needed one. I appreciate that."

I'm sure you do. We have supported your after-work activities or your drug business. "That's nice. My father appreciates your help," Mary said. "How come you never went to college? Isn't there something else you wanted to do besides being an auto mechanic?" Mary asked, hoping she could get him to slip and reveal something.

"You know how it is. College is expensive. Why didn't you go?" Shane turned it back on her.

"I wanted to be a mechanic, but my father never gave me a chance," Mary replied. Sure, it was partially true, but the real truth was her father cared more for Josh. He was getting what she wanted—attention.

"You're good for a girl," Shane teased.

"What?" Mary asked in a louder voice than she wanted. She took in a breath and released it before looking Shane in the eye. "I can find any problem faster than you."

"You can find them, but can you fix them?" Shane was quick to reply.

"Maybe, if given a chance," Mary said.

Shane placed his hand over hers. Mary hid the repulsion and didn't remove her hand.

"Why would you want to get these beautiful hands dirty?" Shane asked before lifting her hand to his mouth and kissing it.

Mary cleared her voice and removed her hand. "Let's eat before our food gets cold." While they ate in silence, Mary thought about Gunner. He'd asked the same question at the station. Was he just flirting too? As she chewed her burger, her eyes strayed to Gunner's booth. He seemed very interested in what his date had to say. He must have said something humorous, because they began laughing. Jealousy set in as she tried to rationalize their relationship. Gunner had never committed to her. He was entitled to date whomever he wanted, but was he sleeping with the other woman too?

"Mary," Shane called. His attention went to Gunner then back to Mary. "Mary." He snapped his fingers to get her attention. "You were miles away. Am I that boring?"

"I was just thinking. I'm good at diagnosing mechanical problems, but it's not what I want to do for the rest of my life?"

"I thought you were staring at that couple in the booth over there."

"Why would I do that?" Mary chuckled.

"He came to the garage the other day. He talked to your father about something."

"Oh, I guess I do know him. He's looking for the thief that stole the Chevelle," Mary lied.

"He's a cop. Why don't you go ask him if he has any leads?" Shane urged.

"No, it looks like he's on a date," Mary said. *There's no way I'm going over there.* "I'll call tomorrow. Let's head out. I'm tired." Mary was about to yawn so Shane would get the hint and take her home when her eyes met Gunner's. When he winked, her temper simmered. *How dare he wink at me while with another woman.* Mary stood to break the lure of Gunner's stare. Shane tossed money on the table, and she linked her arm with his only to make Gunner jealous and let him lead her out of the diner.

***

An hour later, Mary walked through her apartment door and hurried to the balcony to watch the sunset. The sun fell fast, not giving her much time to think of Gunner on a date with another woman or how she would handle her revenge on Shane. He was no match for her physically—she could beat the information out of him. Mentally, he could give her trouble. Shane had lied to her and her father for ten years without any hesitation. Mary doubted anything he told her would be the truth.

It took her thirty minutes to get rid of Shane. When he dropped her off next to her car at the garage, he wanted a goodnight kiss. Mary kept him at arm's length by saying she wanted to remain friends but added she wanted to go slow so that he wouldn't lose interest. Mary didn't want Shane to suspect she was investigating him.

She headed for the living room, plopped on the couch, and reached for the remote. After scrolling through the stations, she saw her television provider offered some free channels for the rest of the month. One station had the western movie she'd seen several weeks ago, and she decided to watch it again. As the man took his revenge on his wife and daughter's murderers, Mary pictured herself in the role. Only, instead of shooting them, she kicked the crap out of them and tied them up. Mary watched it to the end and fell asleep while the credits ran.

Gunfire startled Mary awake the next morning. Still on the couch with the remote sticking in her back, Mary sat up, pointed it at the television to shut it off, then set the controller on the table next to the couch. She reached into her purse for her phone to check the time and saw she had an hour to get to work.

When she was stepping from the shower, the phone rang. Mary wrapped up in a towel before reaching for her phone. It was the body shop—the Chevelle was ready for pickup. Mary made arrangements to pick it up on Saturday. The garage was only open till noon, and they were open till five. That meant she had to get to the bank during lunch to withdraw the cash.

"My house will just have to wait a bit longer," Mary mumbled.

Mary had been saving for a down payment on a house. She didn't care the size, just as long the house came with a large backyard. Mary wanted a dog or cat, any pet to help with the loneliness.

It was two in the afternoon before she could sneak away to the bank. The cost of the Chevelle's restoration took most of her savings, but Mary thought revenge at any price was worth it. She could have just written a check but didn't want them to trace the Chevelle back to her in any way. Mary didn't tell the shop that Gunner had recommended them. All they had so far were her phone number and a made-up name she'd given them—Trinity.

Trinity. The father, the son, and the holy ghost. Mary just hoped God would understand her need for revenge. Three men were responsible for her mother's murder, and three men needed to die. But could Mary kill? Could she break the fifth commandment? "Vengeance is mine says the Lord." *I'm already on the path to hell for sleeping with Gunner.* Hebrews 13:4 said, "God will judge the immoral and adulterers." Mary couldn't remember the entire psalm.

She hadn't kept up with catechism teachings for years. Mary hadn't gone to church since moving out of her father's home. Her father had insisted she go. There were times when the priest's sermons gave her the strength to continue, but after a while, Mary found them hypocritical. *How could God let my mother's murders go unpunished? What happened to an eye for an eye and a tooth for a tooth?*

Chapter Seven

A week had passed since Mary picked up the Chevelle from the shop. She'd spent a weekend and the weeknights learning to drive a manual transmission. She'd stalled the car hundreds of times before learning to shift with ease.

"Look out, Jeff Gordon!" Mary yelled when perfecting it. To minimize the risk that someone would recognize her, Mary only took the Chevelle out after dark. It took a ton of willpower not to show her father how beautiful the car looked, but he could never be involved with her plans for revenge. He would most likely say they should let the police handle it or turn the other cheek because it didn't matter anymore and revenge wasn't worth her life or going to prison. If the bad guys won, and Mary lost her life, she planned to leave the car to Josh. He would've gotten it anyway.

Mary had rented a stall at a storage facility about a mile from her apartment to store the Chevelle. For a quick exit, she backed the car inside. Mary put the car in neutral and revved the engine. Three-hundred-fifty horsepower sounded like a growl of the Kodiak bear. Could the Chevelle outrun the Skylark? If it were 1972, when the car was made, Mary wouldn't worry, but nowadays, people rebuilt their engines. Who knew what was under the Skylark's hood? They had more experience driving a manual transmission, but Mary believed her mother's hand would guide her through it.

"Oh, I almost forgot." Mary reached inside her bag and pulled out the purple box—the present her mother never got to open. She unscrewed the red ball with the worn number three and pulled the new one from the box. She kissed it before placing it on the stick. The moment brought tears to Mary's eyes. She tossed the old pool ball in the glove compartment and slammed it shut.

"I love you, Mom," Mary whispered. She imagined her mother's hand resting over hers as she gripped the ball. "Too bad you didn't get the chance to see it."

Mary cut the engine and stepped out, carrying the empty box. She dropped it in her purse before running her hand over the hood. "I hope you like the color, Mom." The hood was warm from the workout Mary had given the engine. "I bet it feels good to get out that stuffy ol' trailer," Mary said, talking to it like she would a pet, before lifting her hand. She strolled out and gave the car one last look. "My little red devil." Mary laughed as she pulled down the door. "I should've painted that on the car somewhere."

**

A knock at her door caused Mary to jump. It was eleven o'clock. *Who would be showing up at this time?* She strolled over to the peephole and looked through it. "Oh my God, JJ! What are you doing here so late?" Mary screamed as she opened the door.

"The question is, where were you?" JJ asked. "This is the second time I've been here tonight. We were supposed to go out dancing for my birthday."

"Oh, shoot! That's today?" Mary sighed. "I'm so sorry."

JJ held up a bottle of wine and a DVD. "Booze and a movie?"

They walked to the couch and plopped on it. "I'm starving. Have you eaten yet?" Mary asked.

"I ate a banana around ten," JJ said. "My belly was growling."

"Let's order a pizza," Mary suggested.

The delivery man showed forty-five minutes later. They'd drunk most of the wine by then. The over-muscled twenty-two-year-old told Mary he went to the university and only worked the pizza delivering job for the summer. The gorgeous Atlas-like jock had received a full ride on a wrestling scholarship.

"We could have made a porno," Mary said after he left. "A handsome pizza man turns up, and we have a threesome." The two roared as they added different scenarios.

"Wait, Miss Goody Two-shoes…" JJ paused in the middle of laughter. "When did you ever watch a porno?"

"I'm not as innocent as you think," Mary replied.

"Did you sleep with Gunner?" JJ glared at Mary as she waited for the answer.

"Yes," Mary admitted. The alcohol weakened her resistance to secrecy.

"Tell me—is he as good as he looks?" JJ teased, her eyebrows moving up and down.

"Better. Gunner's like a big bag of M&M's," Mary said. "And you know how much I love M&M's." The two broke into laughter again.

"Does that mean you didn't stop at once?" JJ was only joking, but she squealed when Mary admitted they'd had sex twice in one night.

Mary didn't know why she revealed so much to JJ. She blamed it on the wine, but her promiscuous behavior weighed heavily on her mind. Mary held back on telling her friend about Gunner's misstep— they hadn't used protection the first time. Mary just hoped her years of being a good girl—or Miss Goody Two-shoes, as JJ called her—would hold some weight in God's eyes, and she wouldn't have to pay for her mistake. Mary started the movie they'd paused when the pizza arrived, wanting JJ to drop the conversation and focus her attention on the romantic comedy.

Mary opened the pizza box and set it between them. The spicy aroma filled the room, enticing both to eat. Mary wondered if this would be the last thing they ever did together, and she instantly regretted forgetting her best friend's birthday. "I love you, JJ," Mary said. "Sorry I forgot your birthday."

"I love you too," JJ said. "Boy, you must be drunker than I thought."

The two giggled as JJ brushed off Mary's sentiments, attributing them to her having had too much to drink. Mary wanted her friend to know her true feelings if the plan for revenge sent her to the morgue. It was two in the morning before the two called it quits. JJ took refuge on the couch after Mary refused to let her leave. JJ had only drunk half a bottle of wine, but Mary didn't want her to drive under the influence of alcohol and insisted she stay till morning.

In the morning, Mary left for work, leaving JJ fast asleep on the couch. The late-night left Mary in need of a nap before the evening. Today, Mary planned to start her revenge by following Shane and see where it led her. After opening, Mary sat in the chair and fought sleep. Her eyes closed, and sleep overtook her. An hour later, the bell over the door alerted Mary that someone had entered. Mary lifted her head from her arm to find Gunner standing in front of the counter. "Gunner." She yawned. "What brings you here?"

"I tried calling you, but my calls went to voice mail."

"What?" Mary stood and reached under the counter for her purse. When she placed it in front of her, it tipped over, and M&M's spilled out. Mary's face reddened as she sealed the bag and tossed it back in her purse. She retrieved her cell phone and found it wouldn't light up. "The battery's dead."

"Slow day or a late night?" Gunner asked instead of explaining why he'd come.

"Yes, and I only got a few hours' sleep." Mary yawned, feeling the need to explain her laziness. She plugged the phone into the charger before giving him her full attention. "What can I do for you, Gunner? Need new tires?"

He released a sigh before answering. "No, I wanted to ask you out to dinner tonight."

"I'm busy." Mary yawned. "I have plans with JJ."

Gunner looked Mary in the eye. "Why are you lying to me, Mary?"

"I'm not. It's JJ's birthday," Mary lied. She turned away to avoid his stare.

"I was just at your apartment. I spoke with JJ," Gunner said.

"I have a date with Shane," Mary said. It wasn't a lie—she had a date with destiny. Her father came from the garage, interrupting their conversation.

"Hi, back again?" Joe said to Gunner as he wiped his hands on a rag. He tucked it into his back pocket before offering his hand.

"Hello, Mr. Kelly," Gunner said, shaking it.

"Do you have news about the Chevelle?" Mr. Kelly asked.

"No, but we're still investigating."

"Mary's taking it pretty hard. The car belonged to her mother," Joe explained.

"I hear it was some car." Gunner nodded before looking Mary in the eye. "I can see why it would upset Mary."

Mary wondered if Gunner could see the guilt in her eyes. Had Gunner come to tell her he knew she'd been hiding the car all along? Or did he expect her to wait for him to call? It'd been over a week since she'd seen him with another woman. Perhaps he wanted her to know she wasn't the only woman he was dating so Mary wouldn't become serious. "Gunner is a friend from high school, Dad," Mary explained.

"Oh, are you here to take my daughter on a date?" Joe asked, hinting that would make him happy.

"Dad!" Mary gasped.

"I asked her out. She says—"

"I said yes," Mary finished over him. She didn't want Gunner to tell him about Shane.

"Great. I'll pick you up at seven." Gunner said goodbye to her father then left before Mary could argue.

"Glad to hear that you're not sitting at home. I worry about you," her father said. "Why don't you take off early. Go home, take a nap, and get ready for your date."

"Are you sure?" Mary hugged her father, gathered up her belongings, and hurried out the door before he could change his mind. Gunner's surprise visit had put the kibosh on her plan to follow Shane. *Most likely, I would have to wait until after dark anyway,* she told herself. It wouldn't get dark until after nine. That left two hours for the date with Gunner.

After reading JJ's note saying Gunner stopped by and thanking Mary for celebrating her birthday with her, Mary went straight to bed. She fell asleep within minutes of resting her head on the pillow. Hours later, the doorbell woke her. Mary ran to answer the door and found Gunner on the other side.

"You're early," Mary yawned.

"It's five minutes after seven," Gunner said. "Did I wake you?"

"Yeah, can we do this another night?" Mary yawned and scratched her head. "I was up too late last night."

"JJ told me all about it when I woke her up this morning," Gunner said before pushing past her.

Mary closed the door and followed him to the couch, checking out his butt on the way. His jeans were snug and left little to her imagination. She snapped out of it when Gunner faced her. His eyes said he was disappointed that she'd lied to him that morning.

"Why were you here so early?" she asked.

"I don't call ten thirty in the morning early," Gunner said. He took a breath and moved closer when Mary sat down. "Did you cancel your date with Shane?"

"I never had a date with Shane," Mary admitted. "I just didn't want to go out with you. I had other plans."

"So, it's come to this." Gunner shook his head.

"What the hell are you talking about?"

"Small talk. Why are you avoiding me?" Gunner pushed.

Mary got off the couch to move away. Just the smell of his cologne made her want him. She sighed when Gunner stayed put, but Mary didn't like how he followed her with his eyes, as if he were studying her. His attention made her uncomfortable. "Do you think after you sleep with me that I have to sit around and wait for you?"

"Oh, I know. You're upset because I didn't call you." Gunner chuckled. "I've been busy."

"I've been busy too," Mary answered. "I could care less if you called me or not." She walked away and headed to the kitchen.

Gunner followed. Mary opened the refrigerator and took the orange juice from the shelf. "Would you like a glass of juice?" she asked.

"Sure." Gunner smiled.

After setting two small glasses on the table, Mary filled them to the top. She emptied her drink with one quick gulp then refilled it before returning the bottle to the refrigerator. "Here you go," Mary said, handing Gunner a glass. She emptied hers again.

"Thirsty?" Gunner's smile widened. "Drank a little too much last night, hey?" He emptied his glass and set it on the table.

"Did JJ tell you that?"

"No, you falling asleep on the job and thirst told me. Not to mention you were sleeping at seven in the evening."

To avoid his judging eyes, Mary picked up his glass and took it to the sink. She rinsed out both and set them in before facing him. "Why are you here again?"

"You agreed to go on a date, but if it's so repulsive to do so, I'll leave," Gunner said.

"You strong-armed me in front of my dad," Mary explained.

Gunner turned on his heel and headed for the door. When Mary didn't stop him, he halted in front of it and turned to face her. "Why are you so upset with me? I thought—"

"You thought what?" Mary asked. "You thought since I had a crush on you in high school and that you were the first man to make love to me, I was naïve?"

1
2
3

"What the hell are you talking about?" Gunner yelled.

"I saw you with her. You winked at me like a whore. Is she your girlfriend?" Mary returned his anger.

"Who? Oh, you're talking about Stevens." Gunner chuckled. "Skinner called in sick, and Officer Stevens agreed to be my partner for a few days." He walked toward Mary and stood in front of her. "Are you jealous?"

"No, I'm not jealous," Mary answered. Seeing Gunner with another woman had hurt. She'd watched him date girl after girl in high school and couldn't get his attention. Gunner pulled her in his arms and kissed her. She fought him at first, but after a while, she stopped resisting and let Gunner's mouth hypnotize her. His kisses placed a spell on her.

"I've missed you," Gunner whispered.

"Me too," Mary said.

He picked her up off her feet and carried her into the bedroom. As soon as her feet hit the floor, she began to undress. When she made it down to her undergarments, Gunner's naked body wrapped around her. He reached behind her, unfasted her bra, then slid off her panties as he lowered her on the bed.

"Crap," Gunner cursed. He rolled off the bed and hurried to his pants. When he returned, he slid on a condom and continued with the foreplay.

Mary moaned as Gunner placed hot kisses on her skin, starting with her neck and lingering at her breasts. Before Mary could insist he make love to her, Gunner thrust inside her. Not even a minute had passed, and she was screaming with delight.

"Wow!" Mary said when Gunner dropped alongside her.

"It seems I can't get enough of you," Gunner whispered. They lay beside each other for several minutes to catch their breath. "I never plan to sleep with you, but it ends up that way."

Mary's stomach gurgled. "I'm starving. I haven't eaten all day."

"I know of a diner that makes great burgers," Gunner teased.

"That sounds great," Mary said before climbing out of bed.

Gunner's arms wrapped around her as he placed kisses behind Mary's ear. His lips sent tingles down her spine. "I know something that tastes even better," Gunner whispered while nibbling on her ear.

"Gunner." Mary giggled as she moved her head to allow him access to her neck.

His lips worked their way to her lips. He inserted his tongue and pulled her in tighter.

"Wouldn't you rather get something to eat?"

"I'm having my dessert first." Gunner pushed her backward on the bed and pulled her toward him.

Mary wrapped her legs around his thighs while he pressed inside her over and over. As soon as Mary took her pleasure, Gunner pulled himself from her, and his seed emptied on her belly.

"I got to remember to bring more condoms," Gunner said. "It's getting harder for me to withdraw."

"I need a shower." Mary's face scrunched up.

"Me too," Gunner agreed. "I promise not to touch you."

"Okay." Mary squinted and gave him a sideways glance. It didn't take long for Gunner to break his promise. Mary scrubbed his back, and he washed hers. All Gunner had to do was caress her breasts with his warm, sudsy hands, and they were having sex in the shower. Gunner lifted her against the wall and pushed inside her. This time, Gunner didn't pull out at the last second and emptied inside her. It was the best sex Mary ever had. It was exciting and a little rough, but it left her feeling exhilarated—until she realized they'd just had sex again without protection. Mary hurried from the shower, and Gunner followed, apologizing profusely.

"I'm sorry, Mary. I lose all control when I'm with you."

"You had no trouble pulling out before," Mary argued as she began to dress. "Put some clothes on." She picked up Gunner's clothes from the floor and threw them at him. They hit him and landed at his feet. "Please, I can't even look at you."

"Do you know how hard that is for a man? It takes a cool head," Gunner tried to explain as he dressed. "Especially with a woman like you."

"What's that supposed to mean?" Mary fastened her bra and covered the two things that Gunner couldn't take his eyes off.

"You're so beautiful, Mary," Gunner said in a sexy tone.

Mary pulled a blouse over her head and slid on a pair of tight jeans. "Save it for the choir. You had no trouble resisting me in high school. I would've given anything for you to look my way." Mary turned to leave, but Gunner grabbed her by the hand.

"You were fifteen. I was eighteen. I would've got thrown in jail."

Mary pushed his hand away and left the room.

"Please, let's not fight," Gunner pleaded as he followed.

When Gunner grabbed Mary from behind, she moved expertly and escaped his grip. Standing in a karate pose, she faced Gunner. "Sorry." Mary stopped her attack. "We end up in bed every time we see each other. Then we fight. Maybe we shouldn't see each other." As she said the words, she didn't believe them. Gunner's lovemaking was the only thing that made her feel alive. Three times in one night was too much for any normal person. Mary didn't even know a person could perform that many times. Either Gunner was just like chocolate—an addictive crutch—or she was in love with him. The thought of giving her heart to anyone scared the hell out of her.

"Let's go and get something to eat," Mary said to calm things. "My treat."

"Sounds great." Gunner smiled.

Thirty minutes later, they were sitting in a booth at the neighborhood sports bar. Several men were seated at the bar, cheering on the Detroit Tigers.

"They must have hit a home run," Mary said when the crew roared. "Do you follow baseball?" Small talk was better than fighting.

"A little." Gunner smiled as if he knew what Mary was doing. "Football is more my sport."

"Oh yes. Gunner Ryan, the world's sexiest quarterback."

"You think I'm sexy?" he teased.

127

"I meant…" Mary blushed then laughed along with Gunner. "You like to tease me, don't you?"

"Among other things." Gunner chuckled.

The waitress arrived and took their orders. Gunner ordered a beer with his meal, but Mary stuck with ginger ale. She had to stay sharp for later—that was if she could get away from Gunner. People piled in, and not long after, they received their meals. Customers filled every booth. "It's busy tonight."

"It's Saturday," Gunner replied. "I usually work on weekends."

"I suppose you have to arrest a lot of drunk drivers," Mary said. She ate her garlic mashed potatoes while Gunner cut his steak. "I think I could eat these yummy potatoes all night," Mary added when Gunner didn't answer.

"This steak is tender."

Mary ate all the potatoes and the broccoli before trying the chicken. The chef had seasoned the chicken with a sweet whiskey-flavored barbecue sauce. She smiled as she chewed. "This is good."

The guys at the bar were booing at the large screen.

"A bad call?"

"Most likely," Gunner replied. He set down his knife and emptied his glass. "Everything was good." Gunner patted his gut.

"JJ and I eat here every once in a while," Mary said.

"How long have you two been friends?"

"I met her in karate class. She lost her father in a car crash. I lost a mother. She understood my pain."

"I lost my father in a car crash too. That's why I moved home. I didn't want my mother to live alone."

When Gunner revealed something personal, Mary wondered if their relationship was developing into something other than lust. Mary found it honorable that Gunner cared enough about his mother to give up his freedom.

"So she's the woman in your life," Mary said, feeling embarrassed for her jealousy.

"Nothing would please her more than to see me on a date." Gunner looked Mary in the eyes. "My mom would be even happier when I tell her you're catholic."

Mary reddened. "You've told your mother about me?"

"Can I get you anything else?" the waitress interrupted.

"Just the check, thank you," Mary answered. She covered the bill with lightning-fast reflexes when Gunner tried to take it. She handed the bill and her credit card to the waitress. "I said it was my treat." The waitress left before Gunner could argue further.

The wind picked up, and the temperature had dropped since they'd entered. Gunner linked his hand with hers as they walked across the parking lot. When it started to pour, Gunner began to run, pulling Mary along with him. He unlocked her side and opened the door before running around to the driver's side.

"I didn't know it was supposed to rain." Mary shivered.

"The Weather Channel said a forty percent chance after ten," Gunner said before starting the car. "Another month or so, and the rain will turn to snow." He rubbed the water from his arms.

"I was hoping it wouldn't snow until Christmas Eve," Mary replied. "It can melt by New Year's Day."

"Not a fan of the winter?" When windshield started to fog, Gunner turned the temperature button to defrost and warmer.

"Nope. Give me a deserted beach on a tropical island, and I'm happy."

"I agree." Gunner nodded. "But I did go snowmobiling once and had loads of fun." The window cleared, and Gunner put the car in gear.

As they backed out, it began to rain harder. A downpour made it hard to see out any of the windows. Gunner turned the wipers and the defroster to high. They were halfway to Mary's house when the car started to hydroplane. "I'm going to pull in here until the rain slows a little."

They pulled into the parking lot at the park and took the spot closest to the edge. Gunner cut the engine, and the only sound was the rain hitting the car like little pebbles. Lightning flashed and lit up the entire area.

"Well, our date started great," Gunner said as soon as it went dark. He wrapped his hand around Mary's. "Are you scared?"

"What's there to be frightened of? It's only rain."

"I meant, are you frightened of this?" Gunner leaned over and placed a long, tender kiss on Mary's lips.

When his mouth wandered to her neck, Mary found herself becoming aroused and pushed him away. "Let's not get into another situation without protection," she whispered.

Gunner released a breath and backed away. "You're right." They sat and listened to the rain for a few minutes, then Gunner turned on the radio. One of Mary's favorite love songs blasted from the speakers.

"Sorry," Gunner said. "I play the radio loud when alone."

"Me too." Mary giggled. "Leave it up."

By the third song, Mary and Gunner were singing along—loudly and out of tune. Gunner turned down the volume quickly, and the only voice that rang out in the car was Mary's.

"You ass." Mary blushed.

"Do you hear that?" Gunner said.

"What?" Mary listened. She heard nothing but a few raindrops.

"I think it's stopped." Gunner started up the car and turned on the defrosters. "As soon as we can see, I'll drive you home."

The clock radio said it was a few minutes to midnight. They'd been in the car, singing and listening to the rain for over an hour. Mary had planned to take out the Chevelle and follow the drugs. She was hoping to hide and wait for them in this park.

A rap on the driver's-side window drew both of their attention.

"Who the hell is that?" Mary asked. She could tell the person was tall and dressed in dark clothing but nothing else.

"Maybe someone is having car troubles," Gunner said. He opened the window only a few inches. "Can I help you?"

A barrel of a gun poked through the crack. Someone grumbled for the both of them to get out.

"Stay inside and let me handle it."

"But they said both of us." Mary's voice stuttered. Her mother's murder flashed in her head. They'd had a gun too.

Gunner opened the door, and the man outside pulled him from the seat. Mary stayed put not because Gunner had told her to, but because she worried the same thing that had happened to her mother would happen to him. Her heart pounded then skipped a beat when someone knocked on her window and ordered her out. Mary opened the door and stepped out slowly.

"Don't hurt her," Gunner ordered.

The man knocked him in the head with the butt of his gun, and Gunner fell to the wet pavement.

"What do you want? Money?" Mary asked.

"Why were you two spying on us?" the man asked.

Mary's eyes widened as she saw the platinum-blond-haired man who stood over Gunner. "It's you," Mary whispered. Mary could hardly catch her breath. The man who had killed her mother stood before her. The man she'd vowed to kill.

"What the hell is that supposed to mean?"

"We pulled over because we couldn't see to drive. We weren't spying," Mary said instead of answering.

The dark man pushed her around the car until she stood in front of him. Mary glanced at Gunner, hoping to see signs of life. When she saw his chest rise and fall, she knew he was still alive.

"Check out the car. See if she's telling the truth," the blond ordered the other man. Mary could hear the man rummaging through the glove compartment.

"His name is Gunner Ryan. Shit," the second man cursed. "He's a cop." The man held up Gunner's badge and a gun. "I found these in the glove compartment."

"You just pulled over, hey?" The blond pointed the gun at Mary. "Start telling the truth."

"I am. We went out to dinner, and Gunner was taking me home," Mary explained.

"Where's your badge?" He walked closer and started to pat her down with one hand.

"Did you give your date a little tonight?" he asked when he patted her breasts. His hands went under her blouse. "I hate the man to die without a happy ending."

Mary punched him in the face then karate chopped him in the neck. When he fell to his knees, she kicked the gun out of his hands then kicked him in the face. The dark man rounded the car and managed to get off one shot before Mary kicked him and hit him repeatedly until he fell to the ground.

"Take that you, you asshole," Mary spat. Then pain from where the bullet hit her finally registered. She reached down and pulled the shoelace from her shoe and tied it around her arm. "It's not deep." It was only a flesh wound. With a few stitches, she would heal without any surgery.

Mary hurried to Gunner's side to check for a pulse and found it slower than average. He needed help. Mary ran to the car to fetch her cell phone. The contents of her purse were scattered over the seat, and her driver's license had been pulled from her wallet. That meant they knew her name and where she lived. She dialed 911, reported a shooting, told them the location, and hung up without identifying herself.

Mary gathered the contents from the seat, shoved them inside her purse, then flung the strap over her shoulder before checking on Gunner again. He was still alive. Mary picked up the blond man's gun.

Her hand shook as she pointed it at him. "This is for you, Mom," Mary said bitterly. "God, please forgive me." Mary closed her eyes and squeezed the trigger, but the gun didn't fire. A bullet flew past her and hit the window of the car. Mary took cover on the other side, putting the car between herself and the shooter. Bullet after bullet hit the vehicle, missing her as she jumped behind it. Sirens echoed in the distance.

"I called the police!" Mary yelled. "They're on the way." Mary crawled to the back of the car to get a better look. When an engine roared to life, she peeked over the top of the car and saw the black Skylark with yellow stripes coming toward her. It stopped next to the vehicle, and two men got out. Mary stayed hidden as two men loaded the unconscious men in the car then drove from the parking lot at top speed.

"Help is on the way, Gunner," Mary whispered before placing a gentle kiss on his lips. "I love you." Mary set the gun on the pavement next to him and ran from the scene. The warm rain hit her face, covering the tears as she sprinted toward the storage unit. The men knew her identity, so staying hidden was her only option.

Thirty minutes later, she arrived, cold, wet, and tired. She climbed into the Chevelle and headed to her apartment to get clothes and money. Mary parked two blocks from the building so no one could connect her with the Chevelle.

After a warm shower and a change of clothes, Mary cleaned her wound, using four butterfly bandages to hold it closed. Mary stuffed food, clothes, and blankets—things necessary to hide out in a garage—inside two large garbage bags.

Mary wasted no time and hurried before it got light. Tomorrow, they would be looking for her. The nights were getting below fifty degrees, so Mary grabbed a quilt.

Mary worried they might go after Gunner. They'd checked his identity too. She told herself that the police would station someone in his room at the hospital so he would be safe. She backed the Chevelle into the stall, cut the engine, then got out to close the door. The place was pitch-black. Mary felt her way down the car until she found the door handle. "I should've remembered a flashlight." Mary released a heavy sigh then a groan when the door bumped her arm as it closed. Using the flashlight on her phone, she reached into the garbage bags in the back seat and pulled out a pillow and a quilt.

The rain started up again just before dawn, and it poured until after nine. The droplets sounded like marbles as they hit the metal building. Mary thought it was God, telling her he was unhappy with her. If the gun hadn't misfired, she would've committed one of the deadliest sins. Was it out of bullets, or had he clicked on the safety? Or did God not want her to kill? She did her best not to fixate on her mother's murder or the man with blond hair so that she could sleep. The rain, the pain in her arm, and Gunner's chance of recovery kept her awake most of the night. Mary's eyes finally stayed closed from exhaustion.

Chapter Eight

When Gunner opened his eyes, he found himself hooked to a machine monitoring his heartbeat and blood pressure. Sharp pain brought his hand to his head, which was wrapped in a bandage. The pain in his head increased as he sat up. Wincing, he held his head as he scanned the room. His mother was asleep in a chair, a rosary gripped in her hand.

"Mom, Mom, wake up," Gunner called.

Her eyes fluttered open and met his. "You're awake." She hurried to his bedside. "We were worried. Your sister just left." His mother rested her hand over his.

"Where's Mary? Is she okay?"

"Who's Mary?" Gunner's mother asked. "There was no woman with you. I think you must have got hit pretty hard."

"I was on a date." Gunner threw back his blankets and tried to get out of bed. "They must have taken her." Dizziness stopped his departure.

"Stay put. I'll call your partner. He said to call as soon as you woke." She guided him backward until his head rested on the pillow, then she left his side to call Detective Skinner.

While they waited for Skinner to arrive, the nurse came in and administered Gunner more pain medication. The nurse said Gunner's condition was improving, and waking up was a positive sign.

"So, tell me about Mary," Gunner's mother urged once the nurse had left. "How long have you been dating?"

"You would like her, Mom." Gunner's heart pounded as he talked about her. "She's beautiful, smart, and sweet… she's a nice catholic girl." Gunner didn't want to describe Mary in that way, but he couldn't tell his mother Mary was also sexy and sassy and could kick his ass if she wanted. Every word he'd used to define her was accurate. He'd just left out how he felt about her.

"Ryan, you're awake," Skinner said when he arrived. "The whole precinct sends their prayers." Skinner spoke in a loud but happy tone. "Hello, Mrs. Ryan." He nodded in her direction. "I always knew Gunner was a tough guy." Skinner's face changed to a more somber expression after his light teasing. He took a small notepad and an ink pen from his front pocket and began asking questions.

Gunner began by explaining that they'd pulled over in the park because of the downpour. "When the rain lightened up, someone tapped on the window. I rolled it down a few inches, and he shoved a gun in my face. Two men forced Mary and me out of the car at gunpoint."

"And what is Mary's last name?" Skinner wrote down the information as Gunner gave it. "I'll drive to the garage after I leave there. I might catch her there."

"I can give you her phone number. What day is it?" Gunner asked.

"Sunday," Skinner answered.

"If she doesn't answer, try her apartment. Mary doesn't work on Sundays. Call her now," Gunner urged.

"Settle down, pretty boy," Skinner teased.

"They could have her killed her. Don't tell me to calm down!" Gunner yelled as he sat up in bed. He dropped backward when becoming light-headed. He closed his eyes until the dizziness subsided.

"A woman called 911, so she had to be alive at that point. When the ambulance and first unit arrived, you were found unconscious on the ground with a head wound."

"Mary wasn't there?" Gunner became even more worried.

"Forensics found four different blood types at the scene. Three male. One female. One of them was yours, so I can assume two belonged to the assailants." Skinner tucked his notebook back into his front pocket. "One blood type belonged to a known top dog in the Serpent Gang."

"The guy in the morgue was a member of the Serpents," Gunner pointed out. "Could they be following me for some reason?"

"A gang, Gunner?" Mrs. Ryan interrupted. "They're dangerous."

"It's my job, Mother," Gunner said.

"I'll assign an officer to guard your son's room," Skinner said to Mrs. Ryan.

"That's not necessary. Just give me a gun." Gunner sat up, trying to prove he could protect himself. The pain increased in Gunner's head, and he fell backward again. "Thanks. I'm not a hundred percent."

"You're suffering from a concussion, Gunner," his mother explained. "Let Detective Skinner handle it."

"But it's Mary," Gunner exclaimed.

"Some girl finally hooked you, aye, pretty boy," Skinner teased then nodded in Gunner's mother's direction. He made as far as the door and turned at the entrance. "Oh, one more detail. Were you or your date eating M&M's?"

"No, why?"

"We found M&M's scattered across the front seat. I thought they might belong to a member of the gang," Skinner said.

"They must have belonged to Mary. They wouldn't be that sloppy," Gunner replied.

"I'll keep you updated," his partner said before leaving.

"You must care about this girl." His mother stared at him, as if urging him to answer.

"Yes," Gunner whispered. "Can we discuss Mary later? I'm tired."

"Rest. I'll stay right here." Mrs. Ryan returned to her chair.

Gunner could tell by his mother's wrinkled clothes and messy hair that she'd been there overnight. "I'll be fine. Go home and get some rest."

"I'm not going anywhere," she said firmly.

"Please," Gunner pleaded. "You look like you could use a shower." Gunner played on his mother's vanity. His mother never went anywhere unless she looked the part. Perhaps that was one of the reasons he was attracted to Mary—she didn't care about appearances.

"You win. I will leave after you fall asleep," she said.

It works every time. Gunner smiled before closing his eyes. His mother loved him; he would never dispute that. His mother was a beautiful woman, and she knew it.

Expensive clothes, the country club, and a hundred-thousand-dollar car told him she liked material things, but he knew she would choose her children over all of that if it came down to it. When his father died, grief almost overtook her. Gunner wished she would meet another man to fill the void. He didn't want her to spend the rest of her life alone.

***

Mary's eyes opened. She guessed it was daytime because the light in the storage unit was dim. She checked her cell and found it was a quarter after four in the afternoon. Hunger and the urge to relieve herself made her realize she hadn't thought her plan through clearly. She could hide out in the unit, but she needed a restroom.

She pushed off the blankets and climbed out of the car. Pale light shone through the thin fiberglass door. Mary pushed it up and squinted until her eyes adjusted to the sunlight then scanned the area to find no one around.

The pain in Mary's arm returned, reminding her she needed to change the dressing. She had to go somewhere for supplies. Mary swallowed to moisten her dry throat. In the urgency to leave the apartment, she'd forgotten to bring water.

I jogged past a place last night. After locking the unit, Mary stuck her cell in her pocket and walked to the convenience store two blocks away. The business had a clean restroom where Mary did her business before washing in the sink. When someone knocked on the door, she called, "Be right out."

While the restroom was occupied, Mary drank a hot tea and ate a breakfast sandwich while searching the shelves for bandages, peroxide, and an antibiotic ointment. When the bathroom was empty again, Mary returned to change her dressing. She purchased a gallon of water, a flashlight, batteries, a notebook, M&M's, and a newspaper on the way out.

It was after six when she arrived back at the storage unit. There were various people in their own units when Mary returned. She waited until the person in the garage next to hers left. Then she opened the door, put the supplies she purchased in the trunk—minus her chocolate fix—and headed to the front to read the newspaper. Mary plopped on the pavement in front of the Chevelle and leaned against it. The story she wanted to read was on the second page. The article was short. It said the authorities had found an off-duty police officer unconscious in the park, but there was nothing about Gunner's condition.

If Gunner didn't make it, the paper would say. I told him I loved him last night. Do I? Will the police tell my father I'm missing? Will the garage run smoothly without me? What will Shane do? To settle her mind, Mary popped a handful of chocolate in her mouth. *M&M's should be every woman's comfort food.* Mary closed the bag, got to her feet, stuffed it in her pocket, then paced in front of the garage. "Dad has Agnes and Josh. He'll be fine," Mary mumbled. "Gunner has his family. No one will worry about me."

A black car turned down the aisle and headed toward her. Mary ran to the Chevelle, climbed in, and fired up the engine. As it idled at a soft rumble, Mary's hand covered the red ball. "Help me shift, Mother," she whispered.

The car passed slowly, with a family inside.

"You're paranoid, Mary. They don't even know you're here." She cut the engine and rested her head on the steering wheel. It took several minutes for her heart to stop racing. Mary stepped out, walked the fenced-in area, and ate chocolate while she counted the doors. The facility contained fifty smaller units and twenty-five large enough to fit a car. As she rounded the corner, a middle-aged man in an old Ford truck was cleaning out one of the smaller units. He was having difficulty loading an oversized couch onto the truck bed.

"Can I help?" Mary asked.

"Sure, I'll get in the back while you push."

"There's an easier way." Mary helped him lift one end. He picked up the couch, and it slid right in.

"Thanks, your way is a lot easier."

The lifting aggravated the wound, and the pain in her arm returned. "No problem." Mary smiled until facing the opposite direction. Back at her unit, she swallowed a few pain pills and took her usual seat on the pavement in front of the Chevelle. Thirty minutes later, the man she'd helped with the couch appeared, carrying a lawn chair.

"Hi again," he said with a nod.

Mary stood up fast and greeted him with a smile. "Hello. Are you all moved out?"

She studied the man. He looked to be around her father's age, dressed in a plaid flannel shirt over a navy-blue T-shirt. His blue jeans barely covered his ankles, and he'd worn the toes of his leather boots almost clean through.

"Matt." He held out his hand.

She smiled while shaking it. "Mary."

"I have to make one more trip. I think I'll leave the rest till next week." Matt returned Mary's smile. "I noticed you've been hanging out all day." His eyes went to the Chevelle. "Is that your car?"

"Yes, my mother gave it to me," Mary answered.

"Nice. I owned a '69 in high school," Matt claimed.

"Wow, a '69?" Mary's voice rose with enthusiasm. "Doesn't the '69 have square taillights?"

"Yes, you must know your cars." He smiled. "When I sold it, it felt like a piece of me went with it." He lost his smile and released a sigh.

"Then why sell it?" Mary's eyes narrowed.

"First came the wife. Then kids." He shrugged again. "Then came the minivan." He put down the chair and walked around the Chevelle. "Did you do a full restoration?"

"Nope. We've had it in storage." She didn't feel the need to explain the paint job. "Is it against the rules to stay here?" Mary asked to change the subject.

"I don't know. Don't care." Matt shrugged. "I only came to see if you could use a chair."

"You don't want it?" Mary asked.

"I can pick it up next week. If you leave before then, just set it outside your door."

"Someone might steal it," Mary pointed out.

"It's only worth a few dollars." He shrugged as he handed it to her.

"Thanks," Mary said, taking it from his hands. "Beats sitting on the cold pavement."

"See you later," Matt called while walking away.

Mary grabbed an apple from the food she'd brought from home and took a seat. It was nice of the man to think of her. She wondered if Matt had seen the bags and blankets in the back seat and suspected she was homeless. *Why else would he offer the chair?*

Mary read the paper while she chewed, but her mind kept returning to the blond man. *I shot him—or I would have if the gun had fired. I'm capable of murder. What would Father Donovan say? I haven't gone to confession in over a year.* She folded the paper, tossed it in the corner, and walked outside. The sunlight had begun to fade. Mary grabbed the bags from the back seat and set them on the garage floor, leaving the blanket and pillow if she had to sit outside Shane's apartment all night.

As the sun fell below the trees, the Chevelle roared to life. Mary drove to her only lead and parked on the street in front of Shane's apartment building. Within fifteen minutes of cutting the engine, the road was in darkness. Mary lost her patience, pulled the keys out of the ignition, and walked through the parking lot to see if Shane's truck was parked. When Shane came out of the building, Mary ducked behind the nearest vehicle. His phone rang as he was getting into his truck. He talked for several minutes before starting the engine. Mary hurried to the Chevelle, making it inside seconds before Shane drove past. She gave the truck a two-block lead before following. Shane stopped at a liquor store and bought a six-pack of beer. He opened a bottle in the parking lot and emptied it before leaving. When Shane stopped at a traffic light, Mary pulled over and waited.

Shane passed through a neighborhood filled with large two-story homes. About every third house was abandoned, and nature had taken over the lawns. Some were burned or crumbling from neglect. Shane pulled into the driveway of the only house on the street that had lights on and parked in the empty space next to two other vehicles. Mary passed the house so Shane wouldn't think he was being followed and drove around the block before stopping four places away.

Mary cut the engine, climbed out of the car, and walked down the dark sidewalk. Someone came out the side door, bringing the sound of music. The door closed, muffling the rap tune, leaving only the vibration from the bass. The glowing ember of the end of a joint told Mary the person was standing on the porch. The sweet aroma traveled across the street on a light breeze. Mary recognized the scent—the odor of marijuana sickened her.

She waited until the weed-smoking man went back inside before she crossed the street. When the music became unmuffled, she ducked behind the parked cars. Another person came outside. A man's heavy footsteps echoed on the wooden porch. With no idea what car to hide behind, Mary's heart pounded as he walked closer. Light from the car door next to her flooded the area. Mary stayed hidden until he pulled away, then she made a run to the side of the garage. The infamous black Skylark sat inside like a sleeping bear that would attack if woken. Mary went in for a better look, touching the fender to make sure it was real. She went to the back and shined her phone on the license plate to read the number.

Mary left the garage, tiptoeing toward the house without making a sound. Most of the windows were too high for her to peek in, leaving no other option but to climb the steps to the porch. The wooden boards had creaked when the last man came out, so that wasn't an option. *But would they hear it over the music?* Mary decided to take the chance and crept up the steps.

The second board from the top had an invisible wire, and Mary tripped over it. The music inside stopped. Mary heard a commotion and footsteps coming closer. She leaped over the railing as the door opened.

"It's a girl," someone said. Gunfire rang out, hitting the ground next to her. Mary ran as fast as she could, hearing multiple shots.

The moon was only a crescent—the almost pitch-black night covered her escape. The Chevelle's engine roared to life, giving away her location. The lights from cars in the vacant lot flashed on and turned in her direction as she left the driveway. Using the night to keep her cover, Mary left her lights off, made a U-turn, and sped away. She stopped and backed into a driveway of a vacant home.

She sat at an idle with a pounding heart, prepared to punch it if they found her. Shane's truck and a black sedan drove past. To rest her shaking foot, Mary put the car in neutral and took her foot off the clutch. She waited for ten minutes then pulled out, leaving the headlights out until she'd driven a few blocks. When she was sure no one was following, Mary headed back to the storage unit.

***

"Did you catch her?" Miles asked.

"No, we lost her, boss," Shane answered. "We didn't get a good look at the car, but I think it was a Chevelle."

"You think?" His voice rose.

"It's dark out there," Shane said.

"What color?" Miles's brows rose.

"I know what you're thinking, but I told you—someone stole that car," Shane said. "Besides, it couldn't be her."

"Why? Because you've always had a thing for the boss's daughter?" Draco argued. "We haven't seen her since…"

"Since the night she kicked the shit out of you and Lado," Shane teased. "You're just upset because a girl got the best of the mighty Draco."

Draco was a ruthless killer with no conscience. That was why Draco was the boss's enforcer and had been his second-in-command for ten years. No one, not even Shane, wanted his job. Draco enjoyed the killing more than the money. Draco—whose real name was James Drake—was a man without feeling. He'd given himself the name to intimidate others. Tonight, Draco's died dirty-blond hair and the bruises and black eye Mary had inflicted made him look the opposite. "She took me by surprise," Draco said.

When Shane and the others laughed, Draco gave them the stink eye.

"You're lucky she didn't beat you to death," Shane continued. "The girl has a black belt in karate."

"That's enough!" the boss yelled. "I want you to go into work tomorrow and kill the bitch."

"If I kill her at work, there will be an investigation," Shane said. "Draco almost killed a cop."

"Draco, the cop can identify you." The boss looked him straight in the eye. "Go to the hospital and finish the job. Then go to the auto garage and follow the bitch home."

"No," Shane interrupted.

"I told you. Shane's thinking with his dick," Draco said.

"Shane, you kill her," the boss ordered. "Show me that our business relationship means more to you than a piece of ass."

"Are you stupid?" Shane asked, saying his thoughts out loud.

The room fell silent as every person in the room waited to see how the boss would react. The last person to question him had ended up in the morgue. The boss's face showed no emotion. Then without warning, he landed a blow to Shane's jaw.

Shane staggered backward but remained on his feet. "Sorry, boss," Shane said, rubbing his jaw. He cleared his throat then straightened his shoulders. "I didn't mean any disrespect. I only meant we found Mary with the cop. If they both end up dead, the police will connect the murders. I don't want any investigation that will send cops nosing around the garage."

There was another moment of silence as the boss glared at him. He released a breath then turned his attention to Draco. "We have to risk it. Make it look like an accident," the boss ordered. "Take Lado with you."

"Yes, boss." Lado nodded. The side of his face was bruised and puffy from one of Mary's kicks. "I'm game for some payback."

"When will the next batch be ready?" the boss asked. The boss, better known to the rest of the community as Miles Parker, was the owner of two major hotel chains in the Detroit area. He'd built his riches on the backs of people who suffered from addiction. No one would have known just by looking at him that he was the destroyer of families. Miles dressed well, had a wife and kids, and gave to several charities. It was all for appearances—he cared nothing for the community, or he wouldn't get others hooked on crystal meth. Once someone became addicted, methamphetamine wrecked their life. They could develop severe health conditions, memory loss, and brain damage. Some got aggressive and psychotic and would do anything for their next fix.

"Tomorrow night," Shane answered.

"Good." Miles nodded. "Hey, the Skylark's running a little rich. Can you get me in?"

"Do you smell gas?"

"No, it's not idling right." Miles smiled. "You know I don't like it when my car's not running right."

"Carburetor probably needs adjusting," Shane responded. "What time do you want me to pick her up?"

"I have a thing at my kid's school in the morning. How about Tuesday?"

"I don't know the schedule at the garage. Mary's in charge of that," Shane said without thinking.

"Not for long."

Shane recalled when Mary had taken a week off just recently. The phone had rung off the hook, making it hard to get work done. If someone came in to purchase tires, they walked away mad because they couldn't service. Mr. Kelly could hire someone to answer the phone, but no one had Mary's experience. Her death would break Joe. The garage would be chaos if Shane ran it by himself. *What if Mr. Kelly closes?*

"I'll be storing it away for the winter in a month." Miles smiled as he talked about his pride and joy. "Next year, I would like you to look into getting a little more horsepower out of her."

"Have you given any thought to what will happen if Draco kills the girl? The old man won't handle it well." Shane talked as they walked toward the door.

Miles stopped with his hand on the knob, and his smile disappeared. "I think Draco is right. You're thinking with your dick."

"I'm worried the old man won't be able to handle it."

"You've worked with him for too long. You're getting soft." Miles opened the door and exited.

"Draco killed his wife. How much grief do you think one man can handle?" Shane followed two steps behind, knowing Miles was right. He had grown close to Joe and Mary. They were like family. Even though he was only six years older than Mary, he'd watched her grow from a child into a beautiful woman. Any man would have been proud to have her on his arm. Their date hadn't been a real date, but he hoped that, eventually, her feelings for him would change. "I worry he will close the shop."

Miles shrugged. "It will be just like before. The owner will ask you to run it." Miles smiled as he climbed into the Skylark. He started the car and revved the engine.

"It's off a little," Shane agreed. "See you in a few days."

As Miles pulled away, Shane considered giving it all up. He had over three hundred thousand in the bank. It was enough to purchase a home and start a family. He'd pinched pennies for ten years, but what bothered him was the people he'd hurt on the way. He'd seen firsthand how crack affected people's lives. The abandoned neighborhood had once been a thriving area. Part of it was the loss of jobs, but a portion was due to the drugs he and Miles put out on the streets. Men and women left their children and families and stole or killed to get the next fix. Women sold their bodies. Miles took no blame or had empathy for anyone he hurt. As long as the money was rolling in, he was happy. Miles Parker would do anything to keep up appearances, and Shane believed that made the man dead inside.

Chapter Nine

Calls and messages blew up Mary's phone: seven from Gunner, one from JJ, three from her father, and two from Detective Skinner. Mary didn't answer any of them. She had to let everyone think she was dead, especially her father. And it was going to crush him. To allow any of them to believe it was cruel. She hated to do it, but it was the only way to keep her father safe. It was also the only way to stay alive. There was no retribution on the first night. She didn't even get to look inside and see what crimes Shane and his buddies were committing or identify the leader.

Mary listened to Detective Skinner's messages first. In the first, he asked her to return his call and left his number. In the second, he asked her to come to the station and identify her attackers. To play on her sympathies, Skinner said it would help Gunner. JJ hadn't heard about the attack and had only asked Mary to return her call. A few minutes after ten, her father left a message asking if she was sick.

She took a deep breath, and listened to Gunner's messages. The first two were brief, asking her to return his calls. By the sixth message, Gunner's tone had changed from worried to angry. He demanded shc answer, or he was going to leave the hospital and look for her.

"Mary, please call me." The seventh message brought tears to her eyes. "Mary, I love you." Gunner's admission melted her heart. *Did he mean it?*

Light and warmth flooded the stall when Mary opened the large door. The bright, sunny day felt more like summer than a chilly September morning. "Great, we're having an Indian summer, and I won't be able to enjoy it." She took out the lawn chair and plopped in it. "Hell with it," Mary grumbled, getting up from the chair before her butt had warmed it. "I'm going for a drive."

She folded the chair, leaned it against the wall, and opened the trunk. Clothes and food covered the bottom. Mary reached for a baseball cap, placed it on her head, then stuffed everything back in the proper bags. "I can't leave them in the trunk, or I'll be doing this every day," Mary said as she lifted the bags from the trunk. She tied them tight to keep out rodents and placed them in the back against the wall.

Mary pushed her chestnut hair to the top of her head and tucked every strand underneath the cap. The unique shade was a dead giveaway to anyone who knew her. She told herself that no one knew she had the Chevelle. *Unless the thugs from last night could see in the dark.*

She climbed inside, started the engine, and drove it outside to warm up. While closing and locking the door, Mary said a silent prayer that she wasn't making a mistake by exposing herself.

After a quick stop at the convenience store to use the facilities and change the dressing, she took the Chevelle on a cruise through town. At the traffic light, a man in a Mustang winked at her. Mary blushed, gave him a nod, then pushed down on the accelerator. The Mustang kept up with her for two blocks, then the man waved and turned left. The race and the warm breeze made her feel alive again. She turned in to a fast-food drive-through and ordered a burger and a soda. When she handed him the money, the guy who took her order said, "Sweet ride."

Halfway through the burger, her mind drifted to Gunner and the first night they'd made love. Until that night, no man had touched her in that way. Sex with Gunner had lived up to what she'd imagined. His lips were warm and tender, and his lovemaking left her wanting more. *Should I tell him I'm alive? Maybe he could tell my father and warn him about Shane? Should I just go back to work and act as if nothing happened? I handled two bad guys the other night. What if Shane goes after my father and his family to get to me?*

Mary pulled out of the restaurant parking lot with her mind working overtime. Conflicted, she chose to drive awhile, hoping the fresh air would clear her mind. When the car started to miss and sputter, Mary noticed the gas gage was pointed to empty. The engine quit at the entrance to the gas station, and the Chevelle coasted to the pumps. Mary had failed to remember the older vehicles weren't equipped with a low-fuel warning light, but she did remember that high-performance engines needed more octane to run at peak performance. Mary filled the tank with premium and added an octane booster to get more horsepower.

Instead of driving back to the storage unit, Mary found herself in front of the hospital. *It's okay if Gunner knows I'm alive.* Mary pretended to be Gunner's sister so the person at the desk would let her see him. The officer they'd placed to protect Gunner sat slumped over with his eyes closed. Mary tiptoed past and went inside.

"Mary, you're all right." Gunner's face lit up instantly.

The cop outside burst through the door with his gun drawn.

"It's okay. I know her," he said with his hands raised.

"Sorry, Gunner. I don't know how she got past me," he said, putting his gun back in its holster. "Sorry," he added before leaving.

After the door closed, Mary said, "He fell asleep."

"Rookie," Gunner grumbled. "He's supposed to be protecting me." Gunner smiled and turned his attention to Mary. "I might get out of here in the morning."

"Good to hear," Mary said, returning his smile.

"When Skinner said they found your blood at the scene, I thought... Your arm is bandaged." Gunner held out his hand. "Come here."

Mary ambled closer and took his hand in hers. Gunner pulled her closer to examine her arm.

"They shot me, but I got away." Mary volunteered what happened. "I kicked their ass," she bragged.

"Where have you been?" Gunner lightened his grip. "I've... Skinner's looking for you."

"Hiding. The gang knows who I am, where I live and work." Mary sighed. "I'm worried about my father."

"It would be a dumb move for Shane to hurt your father," Gunner said.

"I found his drug house last night," Mary admitted.

"You didn't go there alone, did you?" Gunner reached for her hand, but Mary moved before he captured it. "Mary, they're ruthless. They won't hesitate to kill you."

"I didn't see anything." She shrugged as if it were no big deal. "They had a trip wire on the steps. I set off an alarm."

"Oh my God, Mary," Gunner grumbled. He threw his hand backward and brought his hand to his head. "Promise me you will stay away."

"No, I can't. You know how long I've waited to find the man that killed my mother. I can't let him get away now."

"Tell Skinner. Let him bring him in," Gunner urged.

To avoid Gunner's touch and his disapproving stare, Mary walked to the window and looked out. As she watched the cars on the street, Mary tried to think of a way to sway Gunner to her side. There was none. Mary turned to face him. "Your message said you're in love with me." She walked closer. "Why?"

"I love everything about you," Gunner replied.

"That's not an answer," Mary said.

"Why do you love me?"

"You heard that?" Mary's eyes widened with surprise. "I thought you were out cold."

"No, I was hoping to trick you into admitting it." Gunner laughed at his trickery. "Your stubbornness is one of the things I love about you. Now please come closer so I can touch you."

"I can't."

"I'll get out of this bed." Gunner threw back the covers and swung his legs over the side.

"Okay, okay." Mary hurried to Gunner's side and lifted his hairy legs. The sheer hospital gown barely covered his manhood. Mary blushed as she pulled the blanket over him.

Gunner seized her hand before she could run away. "Thanks for not making me get up." He grunted. "I still get dizzy."

"He hit you pretty hard."

"What happened after that?" Gunner asked.

"I kicked the gun out of his hand before he could shoot you," Mary said.

"Thank you for saving my life." Gunner brought her in toward him, and she didn't resist. His lips barely brushed hers when the door opened. Gunner pulled away quickly. A beautiful woman walked through the door, holding two children by the hand.

"Uncle Gunner," the little girl said.

"You're awake," the little boy said. They both ran toward the bed, and the boy looked at Mary. "Who is she?"

"Yeah, Uncle Gunner, who is she?" the woman teased.

The woman was a little older than Gunner, but there was no denying they were siblings.

"Sis, this is…" He paused as if he didn't know how to introduce her.

"His friend, Mary," Mary finished for him. She offered her hand, and his sister shook it.

"Laura," she announced. "How long have you two been…" She cleared her throat. "Friends?"

"Since high school," Gunner answered.

"A few weeks," Mary answered at the same time. She stepped away to allow the children access to their uncle. Each one hugged Gunner then stepped away.

"Okay," Laura said. Clearly, she was no fool. "Come on, kids, take it easy on Uncle Gunner," Laura said when the boy tried to arm wrestle him.

"Why aren't you rug rats in school?" Gunner asked.

"Uncle Gunner, we don't go to school this late," the girl said.

Mary checked her phone for the time. She'd planned to visit the drug house during the day, figuring they wouldn't be around. "Well, I'll let you guys visit. I'm late for an appointment," Mary said. "Nice meeting you, Laura."

"Don't leave," Gunner pleaded.

Their eyes met before Mary hurried from the room. Laura called out for her stay as she reached the hall. If she turned back now, she would lose her nerve. Mary didn't slow down until reaching the elevators. When the doors opened to the parking garage, Mary's mind was on Gunner and not on revenge. Seeing Gunner with his family had felt weird. His interaction with his niece and nephew told Mary he would make a great father. Until that moment, a father was the last thing she had pictured Gunner being.

Then panic set in when she couldn't find the Chevelle. Mary looked at the number painted on the glass doors that led to the elevators.

"Where in the hell is my car?" Mary yelled when realizing she was on the right floor.

"Need help?" a woman asked.

"No. Thanks for asking," Mary lied. "I see my car over there." Mary pretended to walk toward it until the lady got on the elevator. Then she fell against the cement wall and released her tears. A large truck backed out of space, and Mary saw the Chevelle. The truck had blocked her view of it. Mary wiped away her tears and walked toward it. *What the hell is the matter with me? Mary Kelly doesn't cry when she can't find her car. Gunner Ryan, what have you done to me?*

"Going somewhere?" Draco asked. "She made it easy on us."

Mary stopped when she recognized the two men walking toward her. "What the hell do you want?" Mary played it cool, but inside, her heart pounded.

"Payback," Lado grumbled.

"Payback for what?" As they walked closer, Mary saw the bruises and smiled. "The way I see it, I still owe you another beating."

Draco pulled a gun and pointed it at her. "You think you're so tough. I should have killed you years ago."

"You killed me the moment you pulled the trigger. Taking a mother away from a little girl is cruel, so whatever you do to me doesn't matter," Mary said with defiance.

The glass doors leading to the elevators opened, and the cop who had been guarding Gunner's hospital room walked out. The second Draco's and Lado's attention followed the noise, Mary kicked the gun out of Draco's hand. She sprang into the air, kicking both men at the same time. As the two struggled to their feet, Mary ran to the Chevelle. The engine roared to life. Mary pressed the pedal to the floor. The tires squealed loudly in the garage as Mary made her getaway. The back window shattered as Draco fired at her.

Mary took the turns in the garage as fast as she could. When the exit came into view, Mary thought she was home free—then Draco appeared, standing in the center, pointing the gun straight at her. The tires screeched when she brought the car to a sudden stop. She revved the engine to intimidate him. The car roared like an angry bear, but Draco planted his feet.

"He thinks I won't run him over," Mary grumbled. She put the car in reverse and backed up a few car lengths, but the other guy was rounding the corner. There was no place to go but forward. "You killed my mother, asshole."

With no other option, Mary pushed in the clutch, threw the car into first gear, and pushed the pedal to the floor. The Chevelle charged straight at Draco. He fired at the vehicle, and bullets hit the windshield, missing her head by inches. One shot hit the headrest; the others went out the back. At the last second, Draco leaped into the air to avoid the collision, but he struck the Chevelle's windshield and rolled off to the side.

The girl sitting in the booth collecting the parking fee opened the large metal arm and let Mary pass through before ducking down inside to evade Draco's wrath. Mary thanked her by blowing the horn.

A horn blew at the Chevelle as it entered the street. Mary swerved to miss a truck and almost lost control. The car rode on two wheels for a time then dropped on all four tires with a hefty bounce. Mary's hand slipped off the gearshift. She gripped it more tightly and shifted. Checking the rearview mirror, she saw a black sedan fly from the exit and turn in her direction. She ignored the stoplight and blew through it. Cars stopped in the intersection, temporarily blocking the sedan's pursuit. It pleased Mary when there were no accidents.

"Let's see what you can do," Mary said, pushing on the pedal. By the next block, the car reached one hundred. The speed frightened and excited her at the same time. She weaved around a couple of cars and took the entrance ramp onto the freeway. A sign just before the curve said forty-five. Mary braked and managed to slow the car to sixty. It took a lot of strength to keep the car on the road.

She merged onto the busy freeway, picked up speed, and moved to the far-left passing lane. When the road ahead was clear, she glanced in the mirror and saw the sedan about a quarter mile back, weaving around cars to catch her. The speedometer read one hundred twenty, and the pedal was almost to the floor. Her lead grew, but how long she could drive that fast depended on law enforcement.

"Where's a speed trap when I need one?" Mary complained. If the police pulled her over, she would be safe. They would most likely throw her in jail for speeding, but at least she would be alive. The night of the attack popped into her head. *I should have kept his gun, and then they would have to run from me.* She saw the exit sign that led to the storage units, made her way across four lanes, and turned.

She made a rolling stop at the sign and went left. As she drove across the overpass, the black sedan went by. Mary smiled, knowing she'd given them the slip. Staying under the posted speed limit, she headed for the storage facility. As Mary backed in, she realized that after the attack, she needed a gun. Otherwise, they would kill her before she ever took revenge.

The hood felt warm to the touch. "I gave you a workout today." Mary patted the car like a dog. "Thank you for your help," she said to the car like an old friend. "When this is all through, I'll fix you even better." Mary opened the door and climbed into the back seat to pick up the glass pieces from the rear window. Using the bottom of her shirt like a bag, she gathered all the shards she could fit and stepped out. Mary repeated the process three times, emptying the glass in a pile in the corner, planning to sweep it up later. The glove compartment had a bullet hole. She opened it to inspect the damage and found a bullet lodged in the door. Her eyes went to the red ball. She gripped it like a lifeline, closed her eyes, and released her tears. Mary cried harder when she saw a bullet hole in the headrest. Two inches to the right, and her life would've been over.

"I don't know if I can do this, Mom," Mary whispered to the red gearshift as if it were a communication device linked to her mother. "Get a grip, Mary." She wiped away her tears before stepping from the car. She unfolded the lawn chair and placed it in front of the Chevelle. *Today was another close call.*

Mary wondered if Draco and Lado had come to the hospital to kill Gunner. Or had she surprised them? Did they have a tail on her?

"Didn't think we would find where you were hiding, did you?" Draco stood next to the door with a gun in his hand. Lado mirrored him on the other side.

Mary stood, taking the best position to defend herself. "What do you want? If you are going to kill me, kill me."

"The brave Mary Kelly." Draco chuckled. "I made you that way."

"Are you proud of yourself?" Mary asked. "Why don't you come closer?"

"Fool me once," Draco said. "I know you're a fighter."

"Looks like you don't know how to count," Mary mocked. "I fooled you twice. Once in the park and once at the hospital."

Draco shot at her feet, and the bullet ricocheted off the pavement, hitting Lado in the leg. He screamed and leaped to the side. When he saw the hole in his blue jeans, Lado lifted his pant leg to find the bullet had missed him. "Watch it, asshole."

"Who are you calling an asshole?" Draco pointed the gun at his partner.

Lado aimed his weapon at Draco.

As Mary watched the two argue, she couldn't believe the incompetence. Luckily for her, they were idiots. She didn't underestimate how cold and vicious they could be, though, for she had witnessed Draco's brutality firsthand when he killed her mother and when he tried to kill Gunner.

"Are these guys hurting you?"

They found themselves staring at the end of a shotgun. When Draco and Lado took their attention off Mary, she kicked the lawn chair at Draco and threw the gearshift ball at Lado.

"Run, Matt!" Mary yelled. She ran to the end of the storage building, hearing shots as she rounded the corner. One bullet hit the metal siding that capped the corner and flew through the air. Mary peeked around the building and saw Matt and Lado on the ground. Blood pooled around Lado's head. When Matt spotted Mary, he pointed behind him and began to drag himself toward the stall. Mary ran to help and lugged Matt inside. She went back for the gun then closed the door. "How bad is it?"

"He missed everything vital, but I'll bleed to death if we don't get out of here soon," Matt said, breathing heavily.

Mary checked the wound. The bullet had gone clean through. Mary ran to her bags of clothes and pulled out a cotton T-shirt. "Put pressure on it," Mary said, handing it to him.

"Should I call 911 or drive you?" Mary whispered.

"It will take the ambulance and the cops twenty minutes. When Draco realizes we're inside, all he has to do is open the door or shoot through it."

"You have a gun," Mary pointed out.

"I used both shells," Matt said.

"You only had two shells?" Mary's voice rose.

"Keep your voice down," Matt whispered. "He doesn't know that."

"Who only keeps two shells?"

"My Winchester is old. The shells are hard to find and cost about a hundred bucks a box. Besides, I only need one to take down a deer."

"Can you walk?"

"Yes, drive us the hell out of here." Matt grunted as Mary helped him to his feet. He wrapped his arm around Mary's neck, and she aided his hobble to the passenger's side of the car.

"Crap," Mary cursed. "He will hear the car start and the door when I open it."

"I can hold out. Call the police." Matt moaned.

"Maybe I can drive through it?" Mary acted like it didn't matter, but she worried how much damage smashing through the door would cause. It was shallow—a man's life was more valuable than a car. The Chevelle was like having her mother back in her life, though. She decided not to smash through the door.

"In the name of the father, the son, and the holy spirit," Mary whispered. She made the symbol of the cross before pulling the door open. Mary ran to the car and hopped in. "Trinity is my middle name!" Mary shouted at the same time she turned the key.

The car's engine thundered to life. Lado's body blocked her exit. Mary gripped the red ball, shifted to first, and cringed as the Chevelle bounced over him. She pressed down on the gas and almost hit Draco when exiting the facility. Draco opened fire, sending at least four shots into the driver's-side door. One struck Mary in the side.

"I sure picked a bad day to ask for my chair back," Matt said.

***

The nurses ran to Mary's aid at the emergency room entrance. Matt's blood loss made him weak, and only out of willpower, Mary helped him stand.

"He's the one that's shot!" Mary yelled when the nurses tried to put her on a gurney. Stabbing pain brought her attention to the red stain on her shirt. She lifted the bottom and found a hole just below her ribs. "I guess you're right."

Two nurses caught Mary as her legs went weak. The last thing she heard before losing consciousness was the nurse calling for a surgeon.

When Mary's eyes opened again, Gunner sat sleeping in the chair as her father paced the floor at the end of the bed. Someone had rewrapped the bandage around her arm and one on her side. She looked around at her surroundings and saw no other beds. The nurses had placed her in a private room.

"Dad," Mary whispered.

"Honey, you're awake!"

Gunner's eyes opened as her dad rushed to the bedside.

"We were so worried." He gripped her hand then kissed her on the forehead. "Your friend Gunner is here."

Gunner stood and walked toward her. She wanted to warn him about Draco but didn't want to frighten her father.

"Thanks for coming," Mary whispered.

"Where else would I be?" Gunner smiled.

When their eyes met, Gunner's gaze was magnetic. Mary couldn't look anywhere else—and didn't want to. Her father's question snapped her out of it, though. "Sorry, Dad. What did you say?"

"I can see you have feelings for him." He smiled as his attention went from Mary to Gunner then back to Mary again.

"As I told you last night, I'm in love with your daughter," Gunner said.

"Yeah, but I didn't know how she felt about you until just now." Joe's eyes watered as he looked into Mary's eyes. "You look so much like your mother," he managed before breaking down. "I didn't want to lose you too." He squeezed her hand, turned away to hide the tears, then wiped them away before facing her again. After another kiss on her forehead, Joe announced he was going to the hospital cafeteria to get a coffee. "I love you," he said before leaving.

"I love you, too, Dad," Mary said. It was apparent her father wanted to give them time alone. The worry in her father's eyes said he wanted to stay.

"I love you," Gunner said before placing a warm kiss on her lips.

"I see your bandage is gone." Mary grunted when she lifted her arms to touch his face.

"Yeah, they released me this morning, but I didn't get to leave." Gunner kissed her hand when she touched his face, then he gripped her hand in his. "When are you going to stop this and tell me who's involved?" Gunner asked. His face lost all tenderness.

Mary looked him in the eye. "After I kill every last one of them."

"You couldn't hurt a fly," Gunner said. "So far, they shot you twice and almost killed me."

"Oh my God," Mary gasped. "I forgot to ask. How's Matt?"

"Oh, the man you came in with last night? Add him to your list for vengeance."

"He's dead?" Mary exclaimed.

"No, he's fine, but he could have died." Gunner looked her in the eye. "You need to let the police handle this before someone else is hurt."

"But I haven't even started yet." Mary took in a frustrated breath, and a pain shot through her side. She grunted. "They pursued me."

"There's a red Chevelle full of bullet holes parked out in the parking lot. Did you steal the car and paint it a different color?"

"Yes, I—"

"You've lied to me and your father," Gunner interrupted.

"Lied to me about what?" Joe paused, taking a sip from his cup, and walked toward the bed.

"Your daughter is the one who took the Chevelle."

"You didn't have to take it, honey. It was yours already." Joe looked at Gunner. "No harm is done. I'll call the police today."

"The harm is why she did it." Gunner expressed his disapproval.

"What has she done? Is that why someone shot her?" Joe asked.

"Tell him, Mary," Gunner said. "Or I will."

The room fell silent as her father and Gunner waited for an explanation.

"I took the Chevelle and painted it red."

"Tell us why." Gunner continued to press.

"To hunt down Mom's killers," Mary admitted.

"Mary, let it go. It's not worth dying for," her father said.

"You've been working side by side with Mom's killer," Mary informed him.

"Shane?" Her father chuckled. "You have gone off the deep end. After your mother's death, I would've lost the business if it weren't for him. I could barely function, and he picked up the slack."

"What a saint." Mary rolled her eyes. "I'm going to kill him first."

"Mary, that's against everything we taught you," Joe exclaimed. His eyes watered as he walked toward Mary. "It's not what Saint Catherine's taught you."

"The church has taught nothing. No matter how good you are, it won't save your mother," Mary said, only to shock him. She didn't mean a word of it.

"Your mother was my soul mate, and I haven't lost faith." His eyes pleaded for his daughter to understand.

"What would Agnes say about that?" Mary asked.

His expression changed from disillusionment to anger. "What do you have against my wife? Agnes has tried to include you in our family, and all you do is push her away. Josh too."

"It's like you said, Dad—it's your family, not mine." The bitterness in her tone displayed her disapproval.

"But it could be." Joe released a breath and was about to speak when his cell rang. "Let's talk about this further when you're better. Excuse me."

"Thanks for throwing me under the bus," Mary said to Gunner.

"Someone had to. What your doing is dangerous, and you need to stop." Mary pushed him away. "Come on, Mary, give your father a chance," Gunner whispered. "You never know when you can lose them." He wrapped his hand around Mary's when her eyes watered. "Give me the chance to show you how much I love you."

Mary knew Gunner was right. She'd pushed her father away because finding her mother's killer had consumed her thoughts for ten years. Mary had no life, and Gunner was offering her one. Could she give up her obsession when she was so close? It would mean no more lonely nights, a home, and children. *Unless Gunner only wants sex?*

"I can see some things rolling around in your head," Gunner said.

"Nothing. I'll tell you everything when I get out of here," Mary said, wanting him to quit pushing. "How soon is that? Has the doctor given you any indication?"

"Somebody shot you. Give your body time to heal," Gunner said.

"That was Agnes. She called to see if you were okay," Joe announced when he returned.

"Sorry, Dad. I never gave Agnes a chance." Mary tried to make amends, but inside, she still wasn't ready. It was going to take a while before Mary would allow herself to feel anything toward her stepmother.

"Now, I want you to apologize about Shane," Joe said.

"I can't do that because it's true. I saw Shane with Mom's killers. He has the same tattoo."

"The tattoo on his neck. He's had it for years. It doesn't make him a killer," her father said.

"It's true, Mr. Kelly. We're still investigating, but for Mary's sake, you shouldn't say a word to Shane and let the police handle it," Gunner urged. He looked at Mary. "Like I've been telling your daughter."

"I don't believe it." Joe shook his head.

"You might want to keep an eye on your family. I could ask my boss to place a patrol car outside your house until we solve this." Gunner used a stern tone to get Mr. Kelly to take him seriously. "They killed your wife and shot your daughter." Gunner touched the stitches on his head. "They knocked me out cold."

"I just can't believe Shane would be involved with people like that," Joe said.

"Dad, two days before they killed my Mom, a '69 black Skylark with gold stripes came into the garage. I heard the killer say they got the wrong car."

"That doesn't prove Shane was involved," Joe said. "Besides, the car has been in the shop lots of times."

"Do you know who owns the car?" Gunner asked.

"It's a friend of Shane's," Joe said. "He's never told me his name." He spoke slowly, like a light bulb had come on in his head as he realized what Gunner was saying could be the truth. "I'll ask him who it is."

"No. He may get suspicious," Gunner said.

"Now I know where Mary gets it from."

"Then what am I supposed to do? You can't expect me to work next to a man that was responsible for my wife's murder." Joe's worried voice elevated.

"You've been doing it for years, Dad," Mary pointed out.

"Just for a few more days. No more than a week," Gunner said. "Give us time to set up surveillance." He looked at Mary. "That's if I can get the drug house location from Mary."

"Drugs. My wife's murder was about drugs?" Joe yelled. His attention went to Mary. "And you've been following them?"

"Sorry, Dad," Mary said. "I just couldn't let them get away with it." She held her side. The pain was getting harder to hide. The pain medication had started to wear off, but another dose would make her sleepy. Taking deep breaths seemed to worsen the pain, so Mary took short breaths when telling Gunner the location.

Gunner kissed her on the forehead, whispered, "I love you," and ran out of the room.

"Oh, I wanted to tell Gunner that Shane scheduled an appointment for the Skylark in the morning," Joe said. "Maybe I can catch him before he leaves." Joe ran off before Mary had time to protest, passing the nurse on his way out.

"Where's he going in such a hurry?" the nurse asked.

"To catch someone." Mary grunted, no longer hiding the pain.

"Sounds like you're ready for more pain meds." The nurse injected the prescribed dose into the IV, and relief came almost instantly.

"That's some good stuff you gave me," Mary mumbled. She smiled at the nurse then closed her eyes. "Better than M&M's."

Chapter Ten

Mary's eyes fluttered open. "Crap, I'm still in the hospital."

She'd woken horny and excited after dreaming she was on an island in the Pacific, drinking piña coladas while relaxing under a big umbrella. Mary lusted over Gunner's tanned, wet body as he emerged from the ocean. They got only as far as a kiss before the nurse woke her.

"Good morning, Mary." The nurse's cheery voice rang.

"Morning," Mary mumbled, squinting when the woman opened the blinds to allow the sun to fill the room.

"We have another beautiful fall day," she announced. "Someone told me it's supposed to get to seventy-five today." She walked to a computer cart and pushed it close to Mary's bed. The nurse clipped a device over Mary's index finger.

"When can I get out of here?" Mary asked once the nurse completed her tasks.

"That's up to the doctor. He makes his rounds in an hour."

"How's Matt?"

"Matt?" The nurse's brow met in the center.

"The man that came in with me. I only know his first name."

"Oh yes. Sorry, I can't give you any medical information unless Matt approves it," the nurse explained then whispered that he was recovering nicely.

"Good to hear." Mary smiled. She felt responsible for his injuries but thankful for his help. "What time is it?" Mary searched for her phone.

"Eight fifteen. We put your cell in the drawer," the nurse said. "Would you like me to get it for you?" Without waiting for an answer, the nurse slid the table closer to Mary.

"Thank you," Mary said as the woman was leaving. Mary took the phone from the drawer and saw a message from her father. Disappointed that there wasn't one from Gunner, she held it to her ear to listen. Mary's heart sank when she realized the message wasn't from her father. Draco said he'd kidnapped her dad and Gunner, and if she wanted to see them alive to return his call by midnight. "That was yesterday." Mary dialed the number, and Draco answered.

"You're too late," he grumbled then hung up.

Mary redialed, but he didn't pick up. "He's only messing with me," Mary complained. "He won't kill them until he has me." Mary placed a call to Agnes.

She answered on the first ring, her voice frantic. "Is your father with you?"

"Agnes, yes, he's with me," Mary lied. "His phone died."

"Why didn't he call? I've been calling all night." Agnes's worried voice changed to annoyance. "Why isn't he at work? Oh my God, you've been shot. Sorry, are you okay?"

"I'm fine. Dad had some engine trouble. He's downstairs in the parking garage, fixing the truck right now. He wanted me to call to tell you he will be home in a few hours." Mary didn't want Agnes—or Josh—to worry. She knew firsthand how losing a parent could affect a kid's life, and if she had anything to say about it, that wasn't going to happen.

"Josh and I will come and visit after school," Agnes said.

"Don't bother. I'm checking out soon." Technically, it wasn't a lie. She was leaving to find Draco—and kill him.

"Oh, then it wasn't that serious." Agnes sighed.

"Just a flesh wound." Mary chuckled when remembering a character in a movie. The person got his arm cut off and claimed it was only a flesh wound. "Look, the doctor's here. I have to go." Mary hung up without giving Agnes the chance to say goodbye or ask a question she didn't want to answer.

Mary pulled out the IV and slid out of bed. The pain in her side increased as soon as her feet hit the floor. Holding her side, she hobbled over to the closet and searched for clothes but found the cabinet empty. As Mary ambled over to push the call button to summon the nurse, she spotted a plastic container underneath the bed. To her relief, everything was inside. Someone had cut her pants and shirt in half. The only things salvageable were the socks and shoes. "I guess I'm wearing a gown." Mary turned the hospital gown so that the snaps were facing the front, then she tied it securely around her waist and slid her feet into her shoes.

"Time to leave," she whispered before grabbing the keys to the Chevelle and her cell phone. Mary waited until no one was in the hall before heading to the elevators. Several nurses were in the reception area, busy with paperwork and deep in a conversation as Mary tiptoed past.

The Chevelle sat just where she'd left it—illegally parked in the emergency parking lot with a ticket in the window. Mary plucked it from under the wiper, crumbled it into a ball, and tossed it into the back seat. The bullet holes in the door and windshield and the busted-out back window made the car look like it had driven through a war zone. Mary opened the door and slowly lowered herself inside, using the steering wheel for support. Dried blood covered the door and the carpet. The blood in the passenger seat where Matt had sat pooled in the center but looked dry. Mary resisted the urge to check it. The barrel of Matt's Winchester peeked out from between the seats. Mary picked it up and laid on across the back seat.

Mary started the engine and placed her hand on the dash. "It's time to show them assholes what we can do, my Little Red Devil," Mary whispered as the car idled. The engine growled as she revved it. The horsepower brought a smile to Mary's lips as it fed her determination to seek revenge. "You might look like hell, baby, but you sound beautiful."

Like the Chevelle was haunted by her mother's ghost, the CD player's lights came on, and a classic rock tune blasted from the speakers. "I'll save him, Mom," Mary said as her mother's favorite band played. "I'll save them both."

A wicked idea popped into her head when the tune ended. Instead of going back to the rental unit or home to change, Mary headed toward JJ's.

***

"She'll be here," Draco said.

"We need to clear out. Burn the place down to hide the evidence," Miles argued. "The girl thinks you killed her father and her lover. Why wouldn't she just call the police?"

"She had two chances so far and hasn't called them." Draco smirked. "I killed her mother. She's after me, not you." Draco slid a full clip into his Glock and tucked it into his waistband. He was sure he wouldn't need the fifteen rounds, but he wanted to take every precaution. "You should leave before the bitch arrives. I don't think she has any idea who you are."

"After you kill her and the two in the basement, I want you to burn this place down."

"Won't that lead them to you when they find the bodies?" Draco asked.

"No, I purchased the house in Shane's name. The cops will assume he was behind everything. They will think Shane got rid of them."

"And the cop?" Draco asked.

"He stuck his nose where it didn't belong." Miles smiled, figuring he had every angle covered.

"The cops come after you hard when you kill one of them," Draco pointed out.

"Poor Shane." Miles chuckled, and Drago joined him.

Draco walked through the house and pointed out all the booby traps to Miles. He'd wired the house to explode if Mary used the back or front doors. There was also a trip wire on the stairs leading to the basement. He'd rigged the bottom step with a pressure device in case she managed to get past that. A person's weight triggered it. The second the person stepped off, the bomb would explode.

"I knew I made the right decision by making you second-in-command instead of Shane." Miles smiled at Draco. "You do what it takes to get things done."

"I heard rumors Shane wanted to leave," Draco said.

"Another reason to set him up." Miles grinned.

"What if he talks?" Draco had concerns. Shane knew every detail about Miles's operation. "I could just kill him."

"He won't talk. He knows I have connections inside. I'll miss someone to service my Skylark." Miles's smile faded. "It's a shame. I have never seen a better mechanic than the old man."

"Maybe it's time to get rid of the car as well," Draco said.

Miles stopped and stared into Draco's eyes. "No one messes with my car."

"Just a thought," Draco replied. He held up his hands in surrender. "I won't touch it, but you may want to hide it for a while."

"I put it in storage every winter," Miles said as Draco followed him to his Lexus. "We might want to lay low for a few months. I'm in the process of buying another hotel. The bank is going over my finances. I don't want anything to look shady."

"After we take care of the bitch, I'll tell the boys to lay low for a while." Draco reached in front of Miles and opened the door for him.

"A lot of them are loyal to Shane," Miles admitted as he climbed behind the wheel. "You might have to keep them in line."

"They are more frightened of me than loyal to Shane," Draco bragged. No one would cross him. The man in the morgue had wanted to leave the gang. The guys had nicknamed him "Bear." He was built like a linebacker and had a powerful punch. No one crossed him. Bear's mistake had been admitting to Draco that he wanted to quit and make an honest living. His girlfriend was pregnant. They were expecting a son, and Bear didn't want to raise his child in the drug environment. Bear knew how dangerous cooking meth could be. He'd gotten lucky when the last place exploded. He'd just stepped out onto the porch. A few steps inside, and he would've been a goner.

"They were upset when you killed Bear," Miles said.

"That kept them in line. They won't cross me now."

Miles closed the door, started the car, then rolled down the window. "Call me when it's all over," Miles said, showing no emotion. "There will be a bonus for you."

After a nod of agreement from Draco, Miles closed the window and drove away.

***

Mary limped into JJ's shop, holding her side. Blood had soaked through the bandage and gown. The pain was almost more than Mary could bear. Her karate instructor had taught her how to ignore the pain by clearing her mind of all negative thoughts. It involved concentration and relaxation—but Mary needed to hold on to her anger.

The smell of shampoo, hair spray, and the chemical used to curl hair filled Mary's nostrils. She rubbed her nose, fighting the urge to sneeze, and searched for her friend. JJ's salon had grown over the past three years. JJ employed three additional beauticians, and each had brought customers with them. Mary had thought Jasmine was crazy when she went deep into debt and took out a loan to purchase the place. Mary had never told JJ how she felt because she admired JJ's courage and willingness to put herself out there. That was something Mary, until Gunner, had been afraid to do. The place was booming. Everyone watched Mary as she hobbled past JJ's coworkers and customers. Three customers occupied beautician chairs, and two were under the dryers. JJ gave her customers tips to style their haircut at home, and the customer stepped out of her chair. As soon as JJ finished with the woman, Mary made her presence known. "Can I talk to you alone?"

"Oh my God, Mary." Jasmine gasped. "You're bleeding."

Except for the women under the dryers, the woman's eyes followed Mary. JJ hurried toward her then helped Mary into a chair in the employee breakroom. "What happened? You're wearing a hospital gown. Were you in the hospital?"

Mary told JJ everything.

"You need to let the police handle this," Jasmine said.

"I can't. Draco will kill them," Mary argued.

"You are the toughest person I know. You could take on most men in a fight and win, but, Mary, you are in no shape to take on a drug ring." JJ pleaded for her friend to listen.

"If I don't, they will kill my father and Gunner," Mary said.

"No, Mary, I love you. I won't go along with this!" Jasmine reached inside the front pocket of her smock and pulled out a phone. "I'm calling the police."

Mary jumped out of her seat to stop her. She kicked the phone from her hands then screamed out as pain amplified from her wound. Mary doubled over. Tears poured from her eyes as she faced her best friend. "Please, JJ, I have to do this. You know revenge for my mother is why I pushed myself to be the best in karate."

JJ's round eyes returned to normal. She took in a breath then stepped toward Mary. "Revenge is against everything Sensei taught us. Karate isn't supposed to be used to incite violence." JJ's eyes watered as she guided Mary back into the seat. "I don't want to lose my best friend." Tears ran down JJ's cheeks. "Please, Mary."

"They have my father. They have Gunner."
Mary's eyes met JJ's. "I'm in love with Gunner."

"You've always loved Gunner," JJ said.

"In high school, that was only a silly girl's crush. I love him now." Mary added, "He said he loves me too."

"Okay, okay. How can I help? Do I need to come with you? I'm a little rusty, but I can defend myself." JJ smiled. "You can be Buffy, and I'll be Willow."

Mary's tears turned to laughter. "You remember that?" When they were just barely teenagers, the two had pretended to be vampire slayers. "You're more than Willow." Mary jumped out of the chair and wrapped her arms around her friend. "Your friendship has meant more to me than words can explain."

"Just 'cause Willow didn't use her fists, it doesn't mean she wasn't a badass," JJ said. "I'll have Shanice reschedule my afternoon appointments." Jasmine stepped backward and ran her eyes up and down Mary. "Girl, you need some clothes. Can't kick ass dressed in a hospital gown."

Mary smiled and wiped away the tears with her fingers and dried them on the gown. "I can't go home. They might look for me there."

"Don't have anything here but smocks," JJ said in a disappointed tone. Her eyes widened and glazed over.

"What's the matter?" Mary asked.

JJ's nose wrinkled as if she were about to say something Mary wouldn't like. "I do have something for you to wear, but you won't like it."

"What? I'll wear anything. A smock is better than this gown," Mary said, standing to show everything it exposed.

"I have the costumes we wore to that Halloween party we went to last year."

"The slutty catholic girl ones?" Mary exclaimed. Her expression matched JJ's. "Wait. That will be perfect."

"I'm not going anywhere dressed like a hooker," JJ said.

"We had fun. You even got a date out of it," Mary said.

"He ended up being a rattlesnake." JJ rolled her eyes.

"It's perfect. I was wearing a catholic uniform when Draco killed my mother. I want him to see I'm not the same frightened twelve-year-old little girl when I kill him."

"Mary, I won't be involved in a murder," Jasmine said. "Even if he deserves it."

Mary released a breath. "Okay, but that means you'll be planning my funeral. My father's and Gunner's too."

"Can't you kick the crap out of Draco? Tie him up and leave him for the police."

"JJ, he will have a gun. His banger friends will have guns. I'll be lucky if I make it out alive." Mary stood. "Where do you keep the costumes? It will be better if I go alone. I won't have my best friend risk her life to help me. This is my fight—not yours."

Shanice entered the breakroom in time to hear Mary's words. The room became instantly quiet.

"You need a gun, girl?" Shanice asked Mary.

"What?" Her forwardness surprised Mary.

"I'm just saying." Shanice moved her head flippantly. "You can't bring a knife to a gunfight."

"Who said anything about a knife?" Mary asked.

"What I'm saying is, if you go looking for a fight, girl, you better have the right tools, or you don't stand a chance." Shanice set Mary straight.

"Mary's fists are considered deadly weapons," JJ said.

"Still ain't faster than a bullet." Shanice's cocky voice returned. "Just saying."

"Shanice is right. There'll be more than just Draco. There will be others. I'm only one girl against an army."

"Call the police. The cops like helping white girls," Shanice said. One of Shanice's colleagues yelled that her next customer had arrived. "Be out in a minute."

Feeling defeated, Mary dropped back in the chair, forgetting about her injury. She released a loud grunt and held her side.

"You can't fight in your condition, girl."

"I have no choice. Besides, I left the hospital before they gave me a prescription for pain meds."

"I think I can help you with that. Be right back," Shanice said before leaving.

JJ went to the supply cabinet, pulled a plastic tub from the top shelf, and carried it to the table. "There you go." Jasmine used a bold tone. She dropped the container on the table in front of Mary. "I know how stubborn you can be. No matter what I say, it won't change your mind."

Mary removed the hospital gown without caring who saw her. Jasmine turned her head when Mary exposed her large breasts and private area. "Ain't nothing you haven't seen before." Mary used the same bold tone as Jasmine. Mary took the cotton blouse out of the container, slid it over her naked body, then reached for the plaid skirt. Mary was fastening the tiny buttons on the shirt when Shanice returned.

"You go, girl." Shanice laughed. She took a step back to gaze at Mary. "Woo-wee! Nothing scarier than a white girl comin' at you in a preppy uniform." She gave both Mary and Jasmine a brazen expression then clarified. "Every girl knows you don't mess with them white girls in the private schools. Them girls is mean."

The three broke out in laughter.

"Never thought about it that way," Mary said.

"Here, girl. I brought you something." Shanice dropped a handful of pale-yellow pills into Mary's hand.

Mary examined them closely. "What's Norco?"

"Something you're going to need to take on Draco."

"Do you know Draco?" Mary's eyes opened with surprise.

"In reputation only. Draco's someone you don't want to mess with," Shanice said. "His men are scared of him. Cross him or get in his way and—"

"That's enough, Shanice," Jasmine interrupted.

"Just saying. I got a customer waiting." Shanice made it as far as the door. "About time someone does something. His drugs have ruined a lot of people's lives around here."

"What's Norco?" Mary asked again.

"It's for pain, but it can be addictive, so only take what you need." Jasmine went to the cupboard and took out a mug. Then she went to the sink to fill it with water. "Here, wash it down," Jasmine said as she handed the cup to Mary.

Mary tossed one into her mouth and emptied the cup. "Do they work?"

"Yes, give me one of those." JJ reached out.

Mary took them away. "Didn't you just say they were addictive?"

"If I'm going to die, I want to be free of pain," JJ said.

"Take some aspirin then." Mary stuck the pills into the tiny pocket in her skirt.

"Time to get dressed," Jasmine said as she slipped into the matching costume.

"You always wear it better than me," Mary said with a twinge of jealousy.

"What are you talking about? You look a lot sluttier with those big tits of yours," Jasmine argued. "Especially without a bra. I can see your nipple through the material."

"I don't think they're going to be looking at my boobs." Mary held up her hands in a karate pose. "Say hello to my friends Bessy and Gertrude."

Jasmine laughed. "Is that what you named your tits or your fists?"

"You're not funny, JJ." Mary dropped her fists. They both broke out into laughter.

"Gertrude means 'spear of strength,'" Mary explained.

"I knew a cow named Bessy," Jasmine said. "Whatever." She finished dressing and did the same pose Mary did. "I'm naming my fists Jaiyana and Bruce."

"You can't have a man's name," Mary teased.

"They're my fists."

"Okay, but when Bruce leaves Jaiyana for another fist, don't say I didn't warn you." Mary tied the shirttails at her waist. "What do you think?"

"You look like the biggest slut in town," Jasmine said, keeping a straight face. "What about me?" She copied Mary's style.

"Pucker your lips," Mary said.

"Why?"

"Just do it."

Jasmine turned to the side, put her hands on her hips, then puckered her lips.

"You look like the second-biggest slut in town," Mary teased. They both giggled. "If you're coming with me, you'll need a towel to sit on. The last person to sit in the passenger seat bled all over it."

"Is he dead?"

"No, but you didn't think this is gonna be a joyride, did you?" Mary lost her smile. "Maybe you should stay here, where it's safe." Mary picked up her cell phone and headed to the back entrance. As she walked through the salon, JJ followed, calling for her to stop. Mary only stopped when a group of women blocked her departure.

"What's going on?" Mary asked. Shanice and JJ's other employees, Andrea and Rachele, blocked the back door, and two customers stood at the front.

"Everyone overheard what's going on," Shanice said.

"We want to help," Rachele joined in. "I have a gun."

"Yeah, I want to help too," one customer added. The woman left her spot in front of the door and walked to Shanice's station. She opened her purse and pulled out a Glock 19 and a full clip. "This gun shoots fifteen rounds. It's easy to handle." After inserting the clip, she gripped the gun to show how comfortable it felt in her hand, then she handed the weapon to Mary. "I have the safety on." She showed Mary the safety button. "I don't have an extra clip."

Rachele went to a drawer under the cash register. "I keep this here for when I'm working alone at night." She handed her gun to Jasmine. "It's a Glock 19. Just like Shanice's."

"Why are you girls carrying guns?" Jasmine asked.

"It's scary in our neighborhood," Rachele said. "We had two break-ins last week."

"Yeah, a woman got raped on my block," the customer added.

Shanice's customer took a holster out of her purse. "I use this whenever I take a walk at night. It's a good deterrent when they see Big Bessy on my leg."

"See, JJ?" Mary laughed. "I'm not the only one that thinks the name Bessy sounds intimidating."

The woman helped Mary fasten the holster to her thigh then adjusted the height so Mary could pull it out quickly.

"I take it back," JJ said. "Now you look like the biggest slut in town."

"Yeah, but now everyone will be afraid to call me that," Mary said, placing her hand on Big Bessy. The salon filled with laughter. "What time is it?"

"Three thirty," Rachele said. "Why?"

"I'm going to hit them at sundown," Mary explained. "We have at least four hours before it's dark." Mary held her gut. "I need to feed my belly. I'm so hungry and sick to my stomach."

"It's probably the Norco," Shanice said.

"And the fact I haven't eaten all day," Mary added.

After eating takeout, Mary fell asleep.

"Why did you let me sleep?" Mary complained, rubbing her eyes as she walked out of the breakroom.

JJ was standing in front of the cash register, staring into space. Mary interrupted her daydream.

"You needed the rest," JJ said. "And Shanice forgot to reschedule my last appointment, so I just took care of it."

Shanice placed a piece of paper on the counter in front of Jasmine. It looked like a legal document. "All you have to do is sign it," Shanice said. "But I think you're crazy."

"Let me worry about that." JJ took a pen from the cup next to the register and signed her name at the bottom. "Take care of it for me." JJ's eyes watered.

"What is that?" Mary asked.

"Shanice and Rachele are taking care of something for me."

Mary hurried to the counter, but JJ picked up the paper and hid it behind her back. Mary snatched it from her grip and read it. "What are you doing?" Mary yelled. "You can't give your salon away. I won't allow it."

"It's only in case tonight doesn't go as we would like," JJ explained. "It's not as if they're getting off easy. They'll still have seven years of payments on a ten-year loan."

Mary handed the paper back to JJ. "Gunner said I need to trust the police. They've already shot me twice, knocked Gunner unconscious. I got Gunner and my father kidnapped. I even got a stranger shot, seeking revenge for my mother's murder. Maybe it's time to call the cops." Mary plopped down in one of the stylist's chairs, feeling defeated. The pain medicine had already begun to wear off, and she needed something more potent.

The back door opened, and a black man entered, dressed in baggy jeans and a long-sleeved Detroit Lions T-shirt. He walked straight to Rachele. The young man whispered in Rachele's ear, pulled up his sagging pants, then headed out the door.

"You don't have to call the cops," Rachele said with a wide grin.

"Why?"

"Come with me."

Mary took in a breath, slid out of the chair, and followed everyone outside. Mary's eyes rounded with surprise, and her mouth fell open. There were at least five pick-up trucks, an old Nova in need of bodywork, and an SUV. Men and women of all ages stood in front of their vehicles. Some carried guns, others held baseball bats, and a few had rifles.

"What's going on? Why is everyone here?" Mary asked.

"These people are from Draco's neighborhood," Rachele said. "They want to help."

"Draco's neighbors? Help?" Mary babbled. She was confused because people abandoned half the houses on the block.

"We've asked the police to shut that drug house down," the man said in a bitter tone. "They've done nothing."

"They're selling it to kids," a woman from the crowd shouted.

"We want them gone!" someone yelled.

"Gone!" numerous people screamed.

"These are bad men with guns. They won't think twice about killing any of you." Rapid gunfire, explosions, and people getting slaughtered as they approached the house played in her head like a movie. "I can't let you risk your lives."

When several yelled to let them decide for themselves, Mary shouted over them. "They have the house booby-trapped!" When her warning didn't discourage them, Mary began to believe she may have a chance to save her father and Gunner. And if Draco got in the way, she would kill him.

Chapter Eleven

When twilight arrived, people marched upon the drug house. At first, the crowd began with only the people Rachele had rallied to the salon, but when other neighbors found out what the group was doing, they joined in. There had to be at least a hundred people, too many for Mary to count. As it turned out, more than just the immediate neighbors were sick and tired of the drugs pouring into their community, and they wanted to make a stand. It was Mary's plan, and she felt proud that they trusted her enough to follow it.

Several of the gang members met them out front. Mary had discovered from one of the neighbors that the ring called themselves the Serpents, and once initiated, all members were required to get a tattoo of a snake on their neck. The man also told Mary they'd hounded his son Tyrell then threatened to kill him when asked to leave. Men and women of all races showed their anger with the gang. They carried torches, sticks, and baseball bats and threatened to burn down the house if the Serpents didn't leave. The crowd left their guns hidden and planned to use them as a last resort. A gunfight would only get them killed.

As the mob screamed out their grievances, Mary snuck around the back, hoping to find a way inside to rescue the two people she loved most in this world. Draco had stationed two men at the front and the back doors. Mary didn't see him anywhere. The two men posted in the back stood talking about how loud it was getting out front and wrestled with whether to leave their posts to help.

"Draco said to stay put and watch for her no matter what," one of them said.

So, Draco is expecting me. Most likely, it's a trap, and he's waiting inside. Mary tossed a pebble against the window, drawing both of their attention to it.

"Somebody's here," one said.

The other one shushed him. "Quiet."

Mary crept toward them, jumping over a trip wire at the bottom step. A loud creaking sound brought their attention her way when she landed on the step above it. With lightning speed, Mary drew the gun from the holster and pointed it at them. They did the same.

"It's a standoff," Mary said. "I can pick off one of you before you can shoot me."

"Who are you? Nancy Drew?" the white man asked.

In the darkness, Mary's white blouse stuck out like a neon sign. She could just barely make out either man. When the second man smiled at his buddy's comment, Mary saw only his teeth. With her eyes glued in their direction, she inched closer, taking one step at a time. At the top, she stepped backward. "Are either of you Tyrell?"

"What's it to you?" the white man sneered, giving attitude. "Are you going to pretend to know us so we will drop our guard? It won't work."

"I'm Tyrell," the other guy said.

"Don't tell her nothing," the white man ordered, smacking him upside the head. "Focus on what you're doing."

"I just wanted to tell Tyrell I have no beef with him—or you." Mary planted her feet in the best position to jump over the rail if her plan to divide and conquer went sideways. "I'm here only for Draco," she said, lowering her voice to sound more intimidating. "I also wanted to tell Tyrell that I met his father, and he's out front right now." Mary hoped that once Tyrell heard his father was out front, he would want to leave to make sure his father was safe. It would also give the boy a chance to go without risking his life. "I hope one of your gang doesn't shoot him," Mary added when she got no reply. "Everyone's getting pretty angry out there."

Tyrell took his gun off Mary and started to leave.

"Where in the hell do you think you're going?" the other gangster asked.

"My dad's out there. I won't let someone shoot him," Tyrell explained.

The white man turned his gun on Tyrell. Mary shot the gun out of his hand then leaped in the air, knocking him out with one kick to the head. It was a lucky shot—she'd been aiming for the leg. Mary pointed the gun at Tyrell, but he held up his hands and slowly backed down the steps. "Watch the last step," Mary reminded him. Seeing the man bleeding reassured Mary to carry on. "Two down, one to go," Mary said before stepping over him.

There was another trip wire in front of the door. Mary almost triggered it and would have if she were wearing pants. The cold wire on her bare leg alerted her to its existence. Mary halted, took a step backward, then stepped over it. *What other little tricks do you have for me, Draco? I could beat your ass in hand-to-hand combat.*

Two men came from another room. When they saw Mary, they reached for their guns. Mary swept the leg of the bigger guy, knocking him off his feet. The smaller guy shot at her. The bullet missed her head by millimeters. Mary struck him in the face and chest then kicked him. He went flying backward, his head hit the table, and it knocked him out cold. The taller guy charged at her. Mary moved out of the way, and he fell to the floor.

The man got to his feet quickly and stood in front of her. Hairs wiggled free from his ponytail, and he brushed them away then took a stance in front of her. His eyes traveled the length of her long legs then rested at her chest. The see-through blouse showed everything. Mary ignored his unwanted attention and copied his posture.

"Come on, bitch!" he shouted. He flattened his fists and held them in front of him.

Mary didn't know if he had martial art skills or was pretending, but she stood her ground. "Bring it on," she said through her teeth. "But before I kick your ass, tell me where Draco's hiding."

His eyes moved briefly to a door to the right of him. He wasn't even aware that he'd given away Draco's position. "If you can kick my ass, I'll tell you." He laughed then lost his smile. "I saw what you did to Draco and Lado. It won't be as easy with me. I have a black belt in karate."

"Me too," Mary replied with a hint of mockery, not believing his claim. Mary's lip lifted on one side before she released a chuckle. "Let's see whose sensei taught them better." Mary copied his pose and waited for him to make the first move.

The man had speed, attacking her body high and low. Mary blocked his attacks, but he managed to strike her face. She staggered backward, shook off the pain, and continued.

"Not bad for a girl," he teased. "But I'm not done playing now."

"Oh, was I supposed to try?" Mary taunted. This time, Mary was the aggressor. She gave blow after blow until the blond-haired man dropped to his knees. "Looks like your master didn't teach tae kwon do or jujitsu," Mary said before securing the hit that knocked him unconscious. "I guess I should've asked for Draco's whereabouts."

The win made Mary feel cocky and confident. She had never tried her skills in a real fight, only sparring against other students. Mary hurried to the door on the right, placed her hand on the doorknob, then opened it carefully. Light from the room flooded the top few stairs leading downward. Mary flipped the light switch, and nothing happened. She saw a light bulb hanging from a wire over the stairs and tightened it. The staircase was dim but bright enough to check for trip wires, booby traps, or devices that may tricker an explosion. A gut feeling told her not to go down, that it was a trap, and Draco was waiting at the bottom to shoot her. But the determination to save her father and Gunner compelled her forward. She climbed down cautiously, stopping on a landing halfway down. At that point, the steps turned and descended into darkness. Mary considered turning around, but if Gunner and her father were hurt or tied up down there, her actions had put them there. Mary took a breath, held on to the wooden railing, and took one step at a time. When her foot felt an abnormality on the bottom board, Mary stepped over it. When her feet hit the cement floor, the lights popped on, and Mary stood, facing the devil who had killed her mother.

"You made it past Brutus. You must be a decent fighter." Draco pointed his Glock straight at her. "I see you found my pressure device."

"You're slipping, Draco." Mary smirked.

"You're lucky."

"It would've been nice to take you with me," he replied.

2
0
3

The chemicals associated with cooking meth lined the metal shelves by the wall. Drain cleaner, lantern fuel, and antifreeze were a few that Mary could see. Chemicals had eaten through the stove, and the paint was peeling. The smell urged Mary to sneeze. She rubbed her nose then put it out of her mind, as her sensei had taught her. Clearing her mind was something she'd almost perfected, for the pain of her mother's death was unbearable, and his teachings had made it tolerable.

"How're your teeth, Draco? You look like you lost weight." She tried to get into his head.

"I don't touch the stuff." Draco smiled. His pearly whites told Mary he wasn't lying. Meth would have rotted his teeth.

The only way to stop him was to shoot him. She hid the gun from his view so he would think he had the upper hand. Moaning and footsteps on the cement floor drew her attention behind her. Gunner and her father were gagged and tied to a support pole. She started toward them, but Draco told her to stop.

"You should've let it go. Now it will be your fault that your father and your lover will die along with you."

Mary had never pictured herself as fearful when planning her revenge. Every punch, every chop, and every kick she'd perfected in karate was only to inflict pain on Draco. "Let my father and Gunner go. I'm the one you want," Mary begged.

"It used to be between you and me, but you pushed it too far, and my boss wants everyone dead." Draco stepped closer to her but not close enough for her foot to reach. "Any last words?"

"Okay, you got me, but you're not getting out of here alive. The neighborhood is fed up with you pushing drugs on the people of this community. They will burn the place down."

Draco laughed. "That's what I want them to do. Then I won't have to do it myself." His eyes traveled the length of her body and paused momentarily at her breasts. "I don't get the outfit. Is it supposed to distract me?" Draco winked. "I must say a night with you would be fun."

"Don't you remember, Draco? I was wearing something similar on the morning you killed my mother." Mary sneered. "I wanted it to be the last thing you see before I kill you."

"You talk big, but I can see your body trembling," Draco said. "Even though you took down Brutus, you don't intimidate me." He waved the gun in front of her.

"Who's your boss? Is it Shane?" Mary asked, only to stall. She knew he would never tell her, even if he planned to kill her.

Draco laughed. "If it weren't for Shane, you would have been dead already. The poor boy has got it bad for the boss's daughter."

"Put down that gun, and let's see who does the intimidating." When Draco didn't reply, Mary added, "Or are you a chicken?" Mary clucked a few times.

A rock shattered the basement window and scattered glass across the floor. Mary took advantage of the distraction to land a kick to Draco's body. When he fell on the cement, Draco dropped the gun.

Mary kicked it to the side, and it slid across the floor toward Gunner and her father. Using his foot, Gunner pulled it closer to himself. Draco got back on his feet and faced Mary. This time, Mary could see the fear in his eyes. Mary hit him over and over with lightning speed until Draco dropped to his knees. As Mary raised her hand to knock Draco out cold, he tumbled forward and fell flat on his face.

Mary ran toward Gunner. She ripped the tape from his face then proceeded to her father. "Are either of you hurt?" Mary asked.

"There's a jackknife in my front pocket," Joe informed her.

Mary reached into her father's pants and pulled out a Swiss Army knife. "You're prepared for anything." Mary smiled. She cut the rope that tied them to the pole then cut the duct tape wrapped around her father's wrists. "Sorry, Dad." Mary hugged him.

"I should have supported your efforts," her father said as he squeezed her tighter.

"We need to get out of here and call Skinner," Gunner urged, interrupting their embrace.

"What is this?" her father asked when seeing her gun.

"It's my backup."

"You guys aren't going anywhere." Draco had a gun pointed at them. "Ah, ah, ah," Draco warned when Gunner reached for the gun on the floor.

Gunner straightened then stood in front of Mary, holding her back with his arm. "Don't look so surprised. I stashed a gun down here."

Mary could hear police sirens off in the distance.

"As you can hear, the police are on the way, so give it up," Gunner said.

Mary removed her gun from its holster and placed it in Gunner's palm. His hand tightened around it. With one swift motion, he shot Draco in the heart. Then Gunner wrapped his arms around Mary to block her view of the body. "Don't look, Mary," he whispered. He took Mary by the hand and led her toward the stairs.

"Watch out for the pressure device on the bottom step," Mary warned.

"Did you do all this?" Gunner asked when he saw the bodies on the main floor and the room in disarray. Flashing lights and sirens announced the squad car's arrival.

"No one keeps me from saving you and my dad," Mary said as she followed Gunner to the back door. "Oh, there's a trip wire."

"Too late," Gunner said when he heard a click. "As soon as I move my leg, it will go off. Take your father out of here."

"It might not be linked to explosives. It might only be an alarm," Mary said.

"Go. This is my job." He pulled Mary toward him and placed a kiss on her lips. His hand slipped under her skirt. "Mary Kelly, you aren't wearing underwear," Gunner whispered in a surprised tone. He smiled, kissed Mary again, then pushed her toward the door. "Leave the door open."

Mary followed her father outside. They didn't stop running until they were a safe distance away. The police quieted the crowd, and the people began heading back to their cars. Jasmine waved at Mary before heading in her direction.

Gunner came running out the door. As he leaped from the porch, an explosion blew him and the door several feet into the air. Gunner hit the ground hard and rolled a few feet.

When he didn't move right away, Mary ran toward him. "Gunner!" She kneeled beside him. "Please be all right," she whispered as her hand brushed his hair away from his face.

Gunner's eyes opened, and his hand closed around hers. "I'm okay, Mary. It was only a small explosion." He brought her hand to his mouth and kissed the back of it.

Two cops surrounded them with their gun drawn. "Oh, it's you, Ryan," one of them said before putting his weapon back in the holster. The other officer did the same. He helped Gunner to his feet. "I thought you were in the hospital."

"They released me a day ago," Gunner replied.

"I heard an explosion. Are you trying to go back there?" the other officer teased.

Gunner smiled, but when he had trouble standing, he said, "I think I could use a few days off."

"Is Gunner okay?" Joe asked when he and Jasmine joined them.

"He needs some time to recuperate," Mary said then squinted to read the cop's badge. "Officer Anderson."

Anderson's attention went to the clothes Mary and Jasmine were wearing. "Is there a prep school around here?" Anderson released a chuckle and shook his head. "Ryan, I heard your life is never boring."

"Want to trade places, Anderson?" Gunner teased.

"Care to make a statement?" Anderson said.

"Draco kidnapped Mr. Kelly and me. Draco and two of his gang were waiting with guns at the hospital. I'll come in tomorrow and make a statement," Gunner said.

"And the neighbors?"

"They came to help me," Mary explained. "They were a distraction so that I could save Gunner and my father."

"A girl saved you," Anderson teased. "So, it's true what everyone says at the precinct. You're a pretty boy." Anderson and the other officer laughed.

"When I'm feeling better, I'm going to kick your ass," Gunner said.

"Forensics just arrived," the other cop said.

"There are two live ones upstairs. A dead one in the basement," Gunner informed him.

"You might want to stop them," Mary interrupted. "The front door is booby-trapped, and there's a trip wire on the front porch. Oh, and a pressure plate on the last step in the basement."

"They better enter through the back," Gunner confirmed. "Oh yeah." Gunner pointed to Mary. "She kicked the shit out of the guys upstairs. I shot the one in the basement." Gunner handed him the gun.

"This isn't a standard-issue," Anderson pointed out.

"It was mine. I used it for protection," Mary said.

"I want both of you at the station by nine a.m.," Anderson ordered.

"Make it ten," Gunner said. "I haven't slept in two days."

"Okay, Ryan. You look like shit. I'll hold the captain off until then." Anderson nodded and headed out front to warn his fellow officers.

"Can you stand on your own?" Mary asked once the officers left. "I'll run to get my car. You guys stay put."

"Wait, I'll go with you," Jasmine called.

Only the people that had ridden in Tyrell's father's truck remained out front. They were all leaving when the two dropped back to talk to Mary and Jasmine. "I wanted to thank you," Tyrell's father said. He held out his hand for Mary to shake. "The name's Don."

"Nice meeting you, Don," Mary said.

"Thanks for getting my son out of there."

"He did that all on his own," Mary said. "Oh, and thanks to whoever threw the rock through the window. It distracted Draco long enough for me to kick the gun out of his hand."

"That was me," Jasmine admitted. "I was watching through the window. I thought he was going to shoot you."

Mary hugged JJ. "Thanks for saving everyone."

"I didn't dress like a slut to stand by and do nothing," JJ teased.

"Why are you two dressed like that?" Don asked. "After I saw JJ take down two of the four gang members, I was afraid to ask."

"Good job, Willow," Mary high-fived her.

"Not so bad yourself, Buffy," JJ said. The two giggled. "The crowd took out the other two."

"Willow? Buffy?"

"Long story," Mary answered.

Mary and Jasmine explained everything.

"Draco shot you?" Don seemed amazed. "And you went in there anyway? You're one crazy white girl."

"They shot you twice? How could you even fight?" Tyrell seemed as impressed as his father. They arrived where Don had parked his truck alongside the Chevelle. Four people hopped in the back. "How did you get past Brutus?" Tyrell asked.

"Wasn't easy." Mary touched the bruise on her cheekbone. "He packs a good punch.

Don and Tyrell climbed into the cab. Tyrell rolled down his window. "You must be one badass chick. You're the first person I've known to beat Brutus. See ya."

As they drove away, the people in the truck bed waved.

JJ and Mary waved and shouted, "Goodbye."

Mary started the Chevelle then glanced over at JJ. "So, you got to test your skills." Mary smiled.

"You'd be surprised how it all comes back to you when someone threatens your life," JJ replied.

Mary gave her a scowl that said, "Are you kidding me?"

"Yeah, I guess you do understand," JJ added.

Chapter Twelve

Three weeks later, Shane rolled on everyone to save his skin. He turned state's evidence on Miles Parker and the Serpent Gang. The police charged Miles with distributing and selling illegal drugs and ordering the murders of Gunner Ryan and Mary and Joe Kelly. The story of the affluent hotel owner made local and national headlines. The only thing that bothered Mary about the world knowing of his illegal activities was the harm that it caused his wife and children. The other gang members, except Tyrell, received time for making and dealing the drugs. Mary asked Shane to leave Tyrell's name out of it, because he was only sixteen and Draco had forced him into selling. Shane claimed he'd planned to turn Miles in after he ordered Draco to kill Mary and Joe—and he only agreed to testify to save Mary and Joe from a long, drawn-out trial. In Mary's opinion, the reduced sentence was his only reason for testifying.

At Mary's request, her father had hired Tyrell and Don. Tyrell had his first paying job, which kept him off the streets, and he enjoyed learning a new trade. It didn't take much persuasion from Mary to hire Don. It turned out Don had loads of mechanical experience and had just been laid off. Her father also liked Don's sense of community and his willingness to help others. Joe had offered Mary the job, but she was content working the showroom and helping her father when he needed it.

About a week after the police processed the scene at the drug house, it mysteriously burned down. The police suspected the neighbors, but they couldn't prove it and dropped the investigation. No longer under the influence of the Serpent Gang, the neighborhood began to thrive. Parents and children weren't frightened to use the sidewalks or travel the streets. The residents even started a neighborhood watch so that no one could make or sell drugs on their block again.

***

"Let me see!" Gunner yelled playfully.

"No!" Mary shouted back.

"Come on. Please!" Gunner begged. Nude and aroused, he waited on Mary's bed for her to appear in the doorway. His smile widened when she entered wearing the short plaid shirt and the cotton blouse she'd worn to rescue him. This time, Mary had added knee socks and black Mary Jane shoes. Her hair was pulled up into a ponytail.

"I'm here to rescue you," Mary said in a sexy tone. She stood in an alluring pose, pulled the ribbon from her hair, and shook it loose. Mary kicked off the shoes before placing a foot on the bed. One leg at a time, Mary slowly rolled down the socks to tease him.

"Get over here," Gunner ordered in a sensual tone.

Mary giggled, and her face warmed as she strutted toward him.

Gunner rolled over and reached under her skirt. "No panties. Just like that day. I've fantasized about this for weeks."

Mary moaned as his hand went from her thigh to her carpeted domain. She closed her eyes and gasped when Gunner inserted his finger. After she was hot and ready, he removed his finger, sat on the edge of the bed, and began unfastening the buttons on her blouse. The anticipation of his lovemaking made Mary hornier by the second. She wanted to scream for Gunner to take her before she exploded, but instead, she waited while he undid each button. Gunner pushed the shirt to the side, cupped her breasts, then sucked them one at a time. His mouth wandered to her neck, sending all of Mary's willpower out the window. "Take me now," Mary moaned.

His mouth covered hers, then he lifted her off her feet. When Mary wrapped her legs around his waist, Gunner placed her on the mattress and entered her.

"I love you," Gunner said seconds before Mary released her pleasure.

"I love you too," Mary said breathlessly after he joined her in ecstasy.

Gunner dropped onto her, placing a kiss on her neck. When he rolled over, he brought Mary with him. Mary's breasts were ripe for the picking. Gunner moved the chain from her breast and kissed the nipples. "You're always wearing this," Gunner whispered as he held Mary's necklace between his fingers.

"It was my mothers," Mary answered. "I never take it off." The gold charm had three intersecting ovals.

"What is it?"

"It's a triquetra. Gunner Ryan, didn't you pay attention in catechism class?" Mary asked.

"No, I was too busy eyeing all the pretty girls in skirts," Gunner teased.

"After the way you reacted when seeing me in this skirt, I can believe that." Mary snatched the charm out of Gunner's hand and rubbed it between her fingers. "It's the symbol for the Trinity. The father, the Son, and the Holy Spirit. Also, my middle name."

"Your middle name is Trinity?"

"Yes. Mary Trinity Kelly."

"That's neat," Gunner replied.

"Neat? Nobody uses the word *neat* anymore." Mary laughed.

Gunner slid Mary's blouse off her shoulders, kissing her as it fell. "How about *sexy*?" he whispered after placing a kiss on her breast. "How about *sweet*?" Gunner kissed her other one. "Let's see if Trinity means you can climax three times." Gunner inserted his erection inside her and held Mary's breasts while she bounced on top of him.

Gunner's husky voice, his hip movement, and the warm kisses stirred her lower anatomy. Mary smiled and rocked her hips. "I'm going to enjoy finding out."